The Salvation
Of San Juan Cajon

Michael G. Vail

Cholla Needles Arts & Literary Library
Joshua Tree, CA

This is a work of fiction. Names, characters, places and incidents are the products of the author's imagination or are used fictitiously. Any resemblance to actual events, locales or persons, living or dead, is entirely coincidental.

To Laura and Myra

The completion of a novel is, in many ways, a collective effort. Thank you to the following folks who did so much to help me cross the finish line: Janet Dixon; Tony Dormanesh; Jean-Paul L. Garnier; Benjamin Goulet; Barbara Wu Heyman; Daniel Vaughn; Kent Wilson; Kay Hamann Yeoman; Linda Zamora; and Julie Zimmerman.

PROLOGUE.

September, 1982

The crescent-shaped bay's aquamarine waters lapped at the edge of a vast desert. Just past the shoreline, two dozen weather-beaten skiffs rested haphazardly on the sand in the late afternoon sunlight. Huddled beyond the boats was a collection of makeshift wood frame buildings. Inside the dwellings, the fishermen lay exhausted in their beds. They had awoken before sunup to row out of the bay through the darkness. Crouching for hours in the shallow bellies of the boats, they prayed that a grouper or dorado would become trapped within their nets. Few of these prayers were answered today; most of the vessels returned with little to show for their crews' efforts.

Despite this inauspicious eve, one of the most anticipated holy days of the year had almost arrived. On the following morning, the villagers would observe the Day of the Fish, a celebration whose origins reached back to the pagan rites of their ancestors.

To mark this holiday, a carnival always visited the village. It was made up of an exhibit of transparently fraudulent freaks and a rickety Ferris wheel, purchased third-hand years before in America. For the villagers, though, the carnival was a magical intrusion, a glimpse of the mystery and wonder of the outside world, delivered to their humble community by the half-dozen red and blue trucks which annually appeared on the afternoon before the holy day.

1

While the fishermen slept, the worn-out trucks rumbled past the shacks and stopped next to the graveyard and the church. In the fading light, the carnies erected the Ferris wheel and a large tent made of striped canvas. When these chores were finished, they gathered around a huge bonfire. With no bars or prostitutes here, the men squatted on the bare ground and noisily shared bottles of raicilla.

As his companions passed the moonshine, a young man disappeared into the surrounding shadows. He followed a rutted road past the dark shacks. There was no electricity or indoor plumbing here; the smells of kerosene and human waste filled the air. On this night, he felt sorry for himself. He had been away from his own village for six months, and he didn't get along with the other carnies. They made fun of the fact that he still had no beard to shave. "Maybe it's a girl in disguise!" they laughed, scratching their crotches and leering at him.

"Idiots!" he muttered as he trudged down the empty street, shaking his head in disgust.

At that moment, his foot slipped into a large pothole, sending him tumbling to the hard ground.

A teenage girl sat across the road, in front of one of the unlighted shacks, watching him. She wondered if he had broken something. Yet she was too shy to stand and come to his aid.

He struggled to his feet. "Shit!" he exclaimed as he tried to place some weight on the ankle. He began to bounce about in the dark on his good leg.

The girl giggled in spite of herself.

He stopped. "Who's that?" he asked the night. "Who's cruel enough to take pleasure in my misery?"

"I'm sorry. It's just that you look so funny—hopping around like a jackrabbit."

He bounced towards the sound of her voice.

"Like a jackrabbit, huh?" he repeated indignantly.

"I said I was sorry!" She paused. "Are you all right?"

"I'll live. How could you see me? There's no moon out tonight."

"I can see in the dark," she said.

"Really?"

"Oh, yes. My mother says it's a gift from God."

Or the devil, he thought.

"Can you see my face?"

"Of course."

He leaned closer to her.

"I wish I could see yours."

She glanced back at the shack's open door.

"You'd better go," she said, lowering her voice as she turned to him. "If my father catches us together—"

"Are you going to the carnival tomorrow?"

"Yes."

"That's where I'm from. I'll see you there."

For a moment, he continued to stare in her direction, trying to make out her features. Then he gingerly began to limp down the road in the direction of the graveyard.

After he had gone, she stood and stepped through the dilapidated shack's doorway. It had only one room, and she must step over her sleeping parents and brothers as she moved to her pallet in a corner.

Slipping under a single sheet, she rested her head on a rolled-up blanket and stared at the ceiling. She could make out every mismatched board above her head. As she recalled the young man's handsome face, she sighed. She has never had a boyfriend. A tingle of nervous excitement ran up her body. I'll never be able to sleep, she told herself. She can't wait until the morning comes and the carnival begins.

*   *   *

Dawn broke over the sea in a burst of blinding sunlight. The glare and heat filled the shack's east-facing windows and penetrated its crooked, crevice-filled walls. Even though her father wasn't fishing today, the girl and her mother rose in the dark as usual and began preparing breakfast. The sun rose while the family took their places around a plastic table, sitting on assorted chairs and stools. They gobbled up tortillas and fried fish and sipped coffee from cups with broken handles.

Out of the corner of her eye, the girl watched her father. His skin, tanned by his livelihood, was almost as dark as his black hair.

A large moustache drooped under his nose and over his upper lip. When he set his intense stare on her, she quickly lowered her face.

Like her four younger brothers, she resembled her mother, a tiny figure who sat at the opposite end of the cramped table. The woman's Aztec lineage was evident in her round eyes, long nose and high cheekbones. In order to avoid her husband's glare, she directed her gaze nervously around the table from one child to another.

When they finished eating, the family began to dress for the carnival. The woman and her daughter pulled on their brightly colored Sunday skirts while the man and his sons buttoned up their long-sleeved embroidered shirts.

It was already very hot as the man led his family down the front steps of the shack and onto the dusty road. On top of his head rested a short-brimmed straw hat with a tassel hanging at its rear. When the man spotted a neighbor, he nodded solemnly, causing the tassel to swing crazily behind his back. It was as if an insect hung there, fighting to escape.

The girl could see the carnival in the distance. The canvas tent and Ferris wheel were taller than any other structure in the village; taller, even, than the bell tower of the church. She once again felt a tingle of excitement.

When the Mass was finished, the villagers filed out of the sanctuary and formed a semi-circle in front of the tent. The young priest stood alone in their midst. On a small, low wooden table before him set a metal basin filled with seawater.

As the girl and the rest of her family joined their neighbors, she covered her mouth with her hand. The young man was standing behind the priest with the rest of the carnies. He turned his head this way and that, studying each face in the crowd. She blushed as his gaze passed over her. But she reminded herself that he couldn't possibly recognize her; it had been dark as a cave last night.

"In the name of the Father, and the Son, and the Holy Ghost," the priest intoned, blessing the basin's contents with his upraised right hand, "we celebrate the sea's bounty and thank our Savior for his mercy."

The girl and the rest of the villagers made the Sign of the Cross. The priest lifted the basin in his slim arms. Stepping among the families, he dipped his hand into the holy seawater and shook it from his fingers onto the congregants. She felt the coolness of the water dripping down her forehead and crossed herself again.

Once the priest passed them, the villagers stepped away. Relatives and friends called to one another while the barkers inside the tent shouted their spiels.

"Over here, folks, over here!" commanded a short, fat man with a red bandana wrapped about his large head. "Inside"—he pointed at a flap of black canvas behind him—"is the strangest sight your eyes will ever behold. It's a baby that's half human and half fish. Seeing is believing!"

Near the Ferris wheel, which was already surrounded by those waiting for their turn to ride, two old men appeared. One held an accordion, the other cradled a battered guitar. The pair nodded their wide-brimmed straw hats at one another. Then they started to play. Shouts of exhilaration greeted the simple, rousing sound of the music as it drifted across the lot.

The girl stood next to her brothers while their father passed out pesos to each of them. He glared at her as he dropped the coins in her open palm.

"I don't want to see you talking to any men," he warned her sternly. "You're only fourteen years old."

She watched him silently.

"Did you hear me?" he barked.

She nodded quickly and disappeared into the crowd. As she walked away, she whispered to herself.

"Only fourteen years old?" she repeated disdainfully. "I guess he's forgotten that Mother was fourteen years old when I was born."

She stopped in her tracks. The young man was a few feet in front of her. A cardboard tray full of churros hung from his neck by a length of rope. He handed one of the sweets to a little girl. After taking her money, he adjusted the rope with a scowl. Then he began to walk away.

She hesitated, watching his back.

"Here! Churros man!"

When he turned towards her voice, she stood in front of him, offering a coin.

He handed her one of the sweets, wrapped in a piece of newspaper. As he took the coin, he brushed his fingertips along the inside of her palm.

"Your voice sounds familiar," he said. "Haven't we talked before?"

"Maybe."

"You're the girl who can see in the dark."

"How does your ankle feel?"

He ignored her question. "Now that I can see you," he said, "I know your gift comes from God. The devil couldn't have anything to do with someone so beautiful."

She stared at him, transfixed. This all seemed like a wonderful dream.

"Yes, like one of the angels in heaven." The young man took her hand and squeezed it.

She pulled it away as she glanced behind her. "My father—" she began.

"I can get off for a little while. Will you come and meet me?"

"Where?"

"Over there." He nodded at the red and blue trucks which were parked side-by-side at the end of the lot.

She stared into his large brown eyes and bit her lower lip.

"It'll be all right. Your father will never find out," he said. "I'll see you in a little while."

In a daze, the girl wandered through the carnival. Finding herself at the Ferris wheel, she handed her last coin to the carnie. She was oblivious to the cries of the other riders as they rocked back and forth above the village. The thrill in her heart was much more frightening than any feeling this contraption could produce. She was so distracted that she forgot the churro in the gondola when she stepped off.

Walking alone, she passed the church and the graveyard. Finally she reached the far end of the clearing where the trucks were parked. Moving in the shadows between them, she felt as though she was lost in a maze. She remembered a tale she had once heard of a labyrinth her ancestors constructed in one of their great cities. When the Spaniards arrived, they herded the captured and now unarmed Aztec warriors into the maze, where they were hunted down like animals and slaughtered.

6

Why would I remember that story now? she told herself. The thought unsettled her.

"Hello."

Startled, she turned. The young man stood before her, a wide grin filling his thin face.

"You surprised me."

"Just like you surprised me last night."

He grasped her hand and led her into the sunlight. The trucks separated them from the carnival. Beyond the village, the desert stretched towards a distant range of boulder-strewn hills.

He had spread a blanket on the sand. He kneeled on it. Reluctantly, she sat beside him.

"What's your name?" he said.

"Chimalma."

"I'm Julio."

As he watched her, she glanced away towards the hills.

"You've never been with a man before, have you?"

Swallowing nervously, she turned her eyes back to him.

He put his arm around her shoulder and pulled her to him. Cupping her face in his free hand, he kissed her on the lips. He felt her arms across his back.

"You're so beautiful," he whispered.

He unbuckled his belt and pulled down his trousers. She didn't resist as he raised her skirt above her waist. Their sex was clumsy, quick and without tenderness.

Her father had followed her here. While Julio penetrated her, he crouched behind one of the trucks, glaring at the pair. He was so filled with rage that he could barely see. He raised his face to the sky.

"God, why did you give me a whore for a daughter?" he hissed, between clinched teeth.

When Julio finished, he got to his feet and hitched up his trousers. Chimalma pulled her beautiful skirt over her chubby legs. The sounds of the carnival—barkers shouting, musicians playing and singing, villagers laughing—drifted between the trucks.

"I've got to get back to work," he told her curtly. "They're going to be looking for me."

"Julio..." she began.

"I'll see you later," he said nonchalantly over his shoulder. "I'll find you and say farewell before we leave."

For several minutes, Chimalma remained seated on the blanket, as still as a statue. Trying to understand what has happened to her. She sensed that, somehow, the last few minutes would change her life.

Finally she stood. Instead of returning to the carnival, she crossed the road and entered the empty church. The carnival's sounds followed her through the open doorway.

Moving to the first row of pews, she kneeled and produced a rosary from a pocket of the skirt. Pinching a bead between her thumb and forefinger, she began to mechanically recite the formalized prayers that the priest had taught her.

*   *   *

It was past sunset before Chimalma returned to her family's shack. After leaving the church, she spent the afternoon wandering along the shoreline. Her life had seemed so simple before. There was her family and the sea and the desert. There were the neighbors she had known her whole life, and there was Mass on Sunday. But her life had grown infinitely more complicated, all in one afternoon. She'd been forced to think about right and wrong, about guilt, about love and about herself. Nothing seemed to make sense anymore. It was as if her sex with Julio had left her in the state of an unborn child, uncomprehending and helpless.

While she walked along the bay, she saw the caravan of carnival trucks in the distance, driving away from the village. As she watched, their headlights switched on in the twilight.

"Goodbye, my love," she said aloud. A wind began to rise from the desert.

She paused now on the steps that led to the shack's open doorway. Her father will be angry because she was gone so long. Perhaps he will beat me, she thought. He has beaten her many times before.

It was black inside the shack, but she could see. Her father crouched next to the doorway, waiting for her return. Sweating profusely, a strange look filled his eyes. Chimalma's body trembled as she stared at him. He was gripping a large metal wrench with both hands.

She turned and stepped back down to the road. Her eyes filled with tears. "Why would he want to hurt me?" she asked herself. She began to run. She passed the darkened church and the graveyard. The sandy lot, empty now, was covered with trash.

She stopped running. Ahead, the road disappeared into the desert. She knew it continued for many kilometers. There was a town down the road, with stores and restaurants and a hotel. Railroad tracks passed through the town, and trains stopped at its station. She had heard that the trains traveled all the way to the border with the United States.

She turned back to the village. The tears ran down her cheeks. She knew she would never see this place again. Chimalma turned her back on the village and began to follow the road.

ONE.

February, 1994

The man sat at his desk, staring down at a pad of lined, legal size yellow paper that was filled with scribbled notes. Since the desk's top was covered with an incredible jumble of reports and loose sheets of correspondence, he was forced to rest the pad in his lap.

He had been studying the notes for quite some time. Now he sighed and pushed the chair away from the mess before him.

In his mid-forties, the man had shortly cropped brown hair that was beginning to gray at the temples. Handsome, although not strikingly so, with fine features and a prominent forehead, he wore a bright red tie.

As he leaned backwards into the chair, he raised his hazel eyes and gazed through the open doorway. Outside his office was a large open space that his staff called the bullpen. This area bustled with activity. Staff members were talking on the phones, working at their monitors and standing in front of filing cabinets, flipping through folders.

Just past the doorway, his secretary's phone rang.

Listening to the voice on the other end of the line, her eyes grew wide. Hastily, the woman set the phone down, stood and stepped into his office.

"I know you didn't want to take any calls." She sounded out of breath. "But someone who says they're from CNN is on line two."

"That's okay, Keona," he said. "I'll take this one." As she walked back out the doorway, he picked up the receiver.

"Micah Wada."

"Mr. Wada," responded a young woman in a brisk, professional tone, "I'm Maggie Helms, an assignment editor at CNN's office in Los Angeles. We've heard about the high school you're planning to build in the shopping center. Do you have some time this afternoon to talk with us about it?"

"Sure." He tilted his face back until he was staring at the stained, off-white ceiling tiles above his head. "I hope this will be on camera. The school district's side of the story needs to be told."

"It will be."

"On the evening news?" he said, still gazing overhead.

"Could be. Depends on how fascinating you are."

"What if I'm as mesmerizing as a Pakistani snake charmer?" He slowly enunciated the syllables of each word.

The woman chuckled. "If you bring your cobra with you to the interview, I promise you'll be on prime time."

"It's a deal!" he exclaimed with fake enthusiasm.

As he replaced the receiver, Micah's boss stepped into the doorway. Dressed in a gray business suit, Dr. Hernandez was much older, with a thick body, wrinkled tan skin and wiry-straight white hair.

"Ready for our meeting at city hall?" He sounded nervous.

Micah met his eyes and nodded as he rose. He was quite a bit taller than the superintendent. He removed a sports coat that hung across the chair's back and pulled it on. Then he reached down and lifted the front page of a newspaper from the top of the clutter.

"Did you see the article about tonight's community meeting?" he said as he displayed the banner headline at the top of the page:

Fate of Contentious School To Be Debated

"And CNN just called. They're interviewing me this afternoon."

When he heard this, the old man tilted his wide face forward.

They walked together past the busy workers, pushed open a glass door and stepped into the bright midday sunlight.

"This will be a first—a school facility planner on national TV," the superintendent said as they headed for his Mercedes sedan.

Micah didn't answer. That afternoon's interview wouldn't be the only time he was with someone from CNN. The following day, a well-known correspondent based at the network's national office in Atlanta was flying to Southern California to see him.

But this encounter had very little to do with the new high school—and everything to do with the most notorious episode in the district's history.

A crime that would shock the nation.

Dr. Hernandez didn't know yet about the second interview. Neither did Maggie Helms and the rest of CNN's staff at the west coast office. But they would all learn of it soon enough.

TWO.

March, 1991

When the previous superintendent retired, he left behind a district in the midst of a student overcrowding crisis. Guillermo Hernandez stood out among the applicants to take his place. At each of his previous two districts, the voters approved a bond measure to pay for desperately needed school construction projects.

During his first week on the job, Dr. Hernandez sat down with the Board's president, Myron Richland. They met at a coffee shop in the city's downtown. The restaurant looked like it had seen better days. The carpet was stained, and tears on several of the chairs around the dining room were patched with strips of duct tape. Richland was well known, though, for holding court in a corner booth. He had been coming to the coffee shop since he was a child, when his father was the city's mayor.

"I know how important it is to eliminate the overcrowding as quickly as we can," Dr. Hernandez said, looking directly at Richland. "But putting together a construction program is like assembling a giant jigsaw puzzle. And we're missing the most important piece.

"We need a master planner."

Richland, who was much younger than his table mate, returned his stare with a frown. He thought hiring Dr. Hernandez would be all that was needed to address the overcrowding crisis. At the same time, he realized how little he, or any of the other Board members, knew about building schools.

"Do you have someone in mind?" he said.

"Last year, I attended a conference in San Diego. One of the speakers was a man named Micah Wada. In a community with no vacant land, he's opened a number of new schools."

Now we're getting somewhere, Richland told himself.

"How did he do it?"

"He bought a school from a neighboring district. He converted the district's administrative headquarters into a school

13

and moved the administrators into portable buildings in a parking lot. He convinced the city to let the district use their parks as school sites."

Dr. Hernandez continued to watch the Board president.

"This is a very clever guy."

*　　　*　　　*

When Dr. Hernandez called Micah's office and asked to speak with him, all he told the secretary was his name. She put him on hold for a moment.

"Mr. Wada is going into a meeting. Can he call you back?"

"Tell him I'm the superintendent of the San Juan Cajon School District."

A moment later, Micah was on the line.

"Dr. Hernandez, what can I do for you?"

"We're about to launch a construction program. But we don't have anyone to lead it. I'm familiar with the good work you've done; I saw you speak at the conference in San Diego.

"I want you to apply for our position."

Micah hesitated. Phone calls like this one didn't come along every day.

"I'm very flattered, Dr. Hernandez—"

"Call me Jim."

"But I'll be honest with you. I'm happy where I am. There's plenty that still needs to be done here. I hadn't been thinking about leaving."

"Do you work for your superintendent?"

Micah paused again. "I report to an assistant superintendent."

"If I hire you, you'll be an assistant superintendent," Dr. Hernandez said. "You'll be working directly for me, and be a member of my cabinet."

This was the name for a handful of managers who guided the district's operations at the direction of the superintendent. In California, it was highly unusual for a facility planner to rise to cabinet member status. Micah and his peers were usually excluded from the deliberations of those who made the district's most important decisions.

Dr. Hernandez was offering him an opportunity to implement a major facility program from a position of real authority.

"How does that sound to you?"

"It sounds," Micah said, "like a position that was made for me.

"You see, I'll be the best assistant superintendent you've ever had," he promised smugly. "Or ever will have."

Dr. Hernandez was taken aback by this show of arrogance.

"You're no shrinking violet, are you?"

"A shrinking violet wouldn't have the balls to build millions of dollars worth of classrooms."

"Let's get a few things straight," the old man said, a sudden edge to his voice. "I expect all of my cabinet members to be team players. And to understand that I'm the captain of the team."

"We won't have a problem," Micah snapped, "as long as you stay out of my way."

The superintendent shook his head. In all his years as a district leader, he'd never met such a disrespectful bastard. But he knew he had no choice—he would have to hold his nose and bring Micah onboard.

During his interview for the superintendent position, Dr. Hernandez bragged to Richland and the rest of the Board members about the bond measures that had been approved at his previous districts. But he didn't share what occurred—or, rather, didn't occur—after the elections. Both of the construction programs floundered. Dr. Hernandez was not a facility planner. And neither of those cabinets included someone with the expertise to guide the proposed projects to completion.

Despite the availability of the bond money, only a handful of the new classrooms were ever built.

THREE.

Micah would begin his new job on the day after Easter. As Good Friday dawned, he boarded a flight to Oakland. Until four years ago, he'd always completed this annual getaway with his wife. But since then, he had made the trip alone.

He drove the rental car north through the density and congestion of the East Bay's cities. Soon, the highway crossed San Pablo Bay and rows of grape vines began to surround him, stretching across the flatlands and up the distant hillsides.

He pulled off in Healdsburg and steered past the town square to a little coffee shop. The place served the best BLT sandwich he and his wife had ever tasted. She wasn't normally a fan of bacon and mayonnaise. "That sandwich is flat-out unhealthy," she'd say. "But it's SO good!"

After finishing lunch, he considered taking a detour to a nearby valley where several of their favorite wine tasting rooms nestled along a country road. Without her, though, this side trip didn't sound like any fun. Instead, he got back on the highway and kept driving north.

As he approached the Mendocino County line, Micah turned onto a two lane byway. Almost immediately, it began to climb a range of hills, zigzagging up the sides of grades and ridges; some of the switchbacks were so tight that he had to slow the car to a crawl to turn through them.

When he reached the peak of the tallest hill, the road began to descend into a pastoral valley. A hundred years before, his wife's ancestors were the first settlers to reach this remote area. Ever since, the family had dominated its economic and political life.

In a few more miles, he entered a small town—nothing more than a dozen storefronts and a wood frame two story hotel. His wife's family had invited him to spend the weekend on their ranch just outside of the town. "Your bedroom's ready, like it's been every Easter weekend," his mother-in-law told him over the phone. But this year, he chose to take a room at the hotel.

Once he checked in, Micah lugged his overnight bag up a flight of stairs, dropped it on the bed in his room and returned to the first floor. Because of the holiday weekend, the hotel was full of out-of-towners. Walking back through the spacious lobby, he glanced at the bar, tucked in a corner of the room. Most of the stools were already occupied. Continuing outside to the gravel parking lot, he slipped into the rental car and pulled back onto the road.

Stands of oaks alternated with open vistas and an occasional dairy farm. Soon he spotted an unmarked dirt road. He followed it up a hill until he pulled into an overgrown clearing. Ahead of him was a clump of trees. Despite the shadows their branches threw on the ground, he could make out the shapes of the headstones, clustered among the thick trunks.

He moved slowly between the graves. The oldest markers were closest to the car. The nineteenth century turned into the twentieth under his feet as he continued walking up the rise.

His wife's plot was at the cemetery's edge, bordering a meadow of tall grass and wildflowers. There were blooms of purple, orange and yellow all around her. Next to the headstone, he rested his weight on one knee. All the marker said was her name and the words MY LOVE.

He felt her presence whenever he visited the grave. He reached down, set his open palm on the mound of soil and closed his eyes. In the sky above, a pair of ravens called to one another as they glided over the valley.

*   *   *

Night had fallen when he pulled back into the hotel's crowded lot. He had to circle it several times before another car backed out of a space and he could park. Now there was standing room only at the lobby bar. But as he approached, someone got off a stool and he grabbed it.

The jukebox was playing George Jones, singing "You're Still On My Mind." Next to him, a woman in her fifties with hair that was too red to be natural was telling the bartender how much she liked the way he'd made her Sazerac.

"This is just as good as the ones in Nola," she said, holding up her half-empty glass so he wouldn't miss her meaning.

"Let me try one of those," Micah said.

She turned to him.

"Have you been to New Orleans?" She was wearing quite a bit of make-up, all expertly applied.

"No. But it's on my bucket list."

"If you appreciate a good cocktail, you'd love it."

"Sounds like my kind of town. What's brought you to the valley?"

She pursed her lips, smudging her lipstick.

"I'm on the way to our beach house in Albion. My husband came up last week. He's waiting for me."

"That's only a half hour away," he said. "Why'd you stop here?"

She studied his features.

"Because I was thirsty. It's a long drive from San Francisco."

His Sazerac arrived and he took a sip.

"What do you think?" she said.

"It's delicious. And strong."

"A little goes a long way."

He nodded. "No need to call it that fancy name. Just order 'The Painkiller'."

She set her eyes on him as a wide smile crossed her face.

It wasn't long before they ordered another round.

"Are you a local?" she said.

He shook his head.

"So why are you out here in the middle of nowhere?"

"Maybe I'm on my way to Albion, too."

She grinned at him.

"You're a smart ass. I like that."

By the time they finished their third drink, the crowd at the bar had thinned out.

She stared at him for a moment.

"What are we going to do now?"

"Let's get another round and go up to my room."

He felt her hand in his lap.

"I like a man who knows what he wants," she whispered into his ear.

FOUR.

Just over one year after Micah's arrival, the community's voters, convinced that the school overcrowding crisis was real, approved San Juan Cajon's bond by a landslide. They were driven to vote "yes" by the campaign slogans plastered on utility poles and staked in front yards: "OVERCROWDED SCHOOLS = A CITY WITHOUT A FUTURE" and "SAVE SAN JUAN CAJON!"

Once the measure passed, it was all-important to find sites for the new schools. Every day, Micah drove a different section of the city, searching fruitlessly for vacant land. The assistant superintendent also contacted numerous Realtors. When he told them the district needed undeveloped property, their response was not encouraging.

"I've worked in this town for thirty years," said one of the agents. "What you're looking for doesn't exist."

One morning, Micah was passing through one of the city's most densely populated neighborhoods when he slammed on the car's brakes. Abutting a city park was what appeared to be a vacant parcel. Full of weeds, scrub brush and dead trees, it seemed to be abandoned.

He spotted a faded wooden sign at the edge of the land that made him begin to laugh out loud. It read NATURE CENTER.

Parking his red BMW, he began walking around the property, which was surrounded by a rusted chain-link fence, its support posts leaning this way and that. A few steps from the car, he came upon a gaping hole. He bent down and began to squeeze through. As he did so, the back of his pricey Italian suit coat became caught on the jagged edges where the fence had been cut. He could hear the cloth ripping.

"Fuck!" he shouted.

He finally freed himself. Pushing his way through the underbrush, Micah saw signs of other visitors. Empty beer cans and whiskey bottles, used condoms and shell casings littered the ground.

Soon he emerged into a clearing. The fence that once separated it from the adjacent street had disappeared; only a few lonely posts remained. There were multiple tire tracks in the dust.

On the far side stood a small, simple wood frame house and, one hundred feet behind it, a large barn. Odd pieces of plywood had been nailed over the buildings' doorways and window frames. The original paint on both had peeled away long ago. In its place were long, jagged black lines of graffiti, representing letters and numbers that seemed to be meaningless.

Back at his office, Micah took off the torn coat and hung it on the back of his chair. Then he phoned the city's land use planner, Judy Gonzalez.

Several weeks before, he was invited by Don Smith, the city manager, to review the district's construction program with the municipality's management team. Before the meeting began, Judy stepped over to him and introduced herself. "I'll be the one to call when you need something from the city," she explained.

"In that case," he said with a sly smile, "we're going to get to know each other very well."

At the end of the meeting, she led him out of city hall and down the street to a nearby bar. When they reached its entrance, he peered at a small neon sign hanging overhead and snickered under his breath.

"Monkey Bar?" he read aloud.

"Don't laugh." She pretended to be offended. "This isn't just a dive bar. This is the MB!"

High on the wall opposite the bartender, a slogan had been stenciled across the inside of the windowless room in large Celtic script: COME ON IN AND MONKEY AROUND.

"I'm beginning to feel the MB's aura," he shouted over the jukebox's ruckus.

She smiled at him approvingly. "Let me get the first round of drinks. Is rum and Coke okay?"

"Sure."

They spent several hours in the place. It was enough time for both to decide that Guns N' Roses needed to record a new version of "Welcome to the Jungle". With a new title: "Welcome to the Monkey Bar".

"The MB will be forever grateful!" she predicted.

"Judy, I'm calling to take you up on your offer of help," he said into the phone. "I was driving by Pearson Park. Searching for parcels the district could use to build new schools. I found an abandoned piece of property."

"If this is the land with the old house and barn, you've stumbled onto an important part of the city's history. The Grimm family established the area's first farm there in the 1920's.

"The property you saw was originally part of a much larger parcel. The family sold most of the land in the 1950's to a homebuilder. There's six acres left."

Almost large enough to build an elementary school, he thought.

"The property isn't abandoned," she said. "It's still owned by the family."

"I saw a sign that didn't fit in with its surroundings."

"The one that says 'Nature Center'? That's the butt of a lot of jokes around here. There's definitely been two-legged wildlife spotted on the place—especially on Saturday nights.

"The family members put up that sign. Their dream is to have gardens and walking trails on the site. To open the restored house for tours and hold community events in the barn.

"Their hearts are in the right place. And the city supports their goals. But...they don't really know what they're doing. I doubt if they'll ever get the restoration off the ground."

"How would I get hold of the property owners?" he said.

"Two sisters, Sarah and Gail Grimm, represent the family's interests."

"Can you give me their phone numbers?"

"Sure. They have the same number. They live together."

She flipped through the Rolodex on her desk, found the number and recited it into the receiver.

Judy paused. "I want you to know something. They're very passionate about the property. They were born and raised there."

"Mind if I call you again?" Micah said.

"Not at all. I'll be glad to help you, if I can."

FIVE.

It was well past midnight as the seventeen-year-old Latino steered his beat-up little Datsun slowly through the darkened residential neighborhood. Only half of the street lamps on this particular block worked; the majority of the residents were immigrants from Mexico who didn't vote, so it was easy for the City Council to ignore their needs.

The driver had been partying with his friends for hours. But there was still one joint left in his shirt pocket, and he wanted to smoke it before he went home and had to face his parents.

Up ahead, nestled in the midst of the modest houses, was the old Grimm farmstead. He slowed the car to a crawl as an Ice-T track blasted from the speakers, mounted where the back seat used to be. Everything looked okay; there weren't any other vehicles in sight.

What he missed in the darkness was the faint glow of a lighter, heating a crystal meth pipe's glass bowl.

The stoned teenager maneuvered the Datsun onto the parcel. Ahead were the boarded-up wooden buildings, vague outlines in his headlights.

As the lights swept across the lot, their illumination abruptly fell

Upon three apparitions

Facing the car

In black T-shirts

With shaved heads

Arms and necks and skulls

Covered

In crude tattoos

Because of the marijuana-induced haze, he wasn't sure at first that the figures were real.

But they were—all too real.

As real as the violent rap that was spitting from the speakers.

"Hail Mary, full of grace," he whispered.

At the open window now, he was face-to-face with a bald skull, seeming to float in the blackness like a balloon with the face of Satan painted on its surface.

The gang member hissed, rattlesnake-like:

"Who you claim?"

"NOBODY!"

Red ink tears ran down the gangster's cheeks, as if he was sad to hear the teenager's lie.

"You bang?"

"I'M WITH NOBODY, MAN!"

A gray pistol appeared and he grasped their plan—make sure he ended the night in a body bag.

Nope, he told himself. It ain't gonna happen. Ain't gonna be me who goes down tonight.

He stomped on the gas pedal. The rear tires began spinning in the dust—and the gunfire exploded. Shells whistled and pinged while the Datsun fishtailed across the lot. The rear window blew out, sending glass shards spraying into his hair and everywhere.

Suddenly his ride bounded off the curb with a boom, landing on the street's asphalt. Tires squealed while shots kept ringing out and he kept praying:

"Deliver me from evil and gimme shelter."

Round a curve and the taillights disappeared while Ice-T kept cursing at the night, the sound of his anger finally fading into the blackness.

One of the gang members produced the meth pipe again and heated the bowl. While he sucked the fumes out, the trio began to walk nonchalantly across the farmstead towards the nearby houses.

SIX.

When Micah dialed the number Judy had given him, Sarah Grimm answered the phone. He introduced himself and asked if he could meet with her and her sister.

"Why do you want to see us?"

"The district is searching for future school sites. I'd like to talk with you about your farm property. Can I come by tomorrow afternoon?"

"I suppose so." She sounded impatient, and perhaps angry.

The sisters lived in a large, well-kept single story house a mile or so from the farm site. Micah assumed it was built for the family by the developer who purchased most of their property.

When he rang the doorbell, an elderly woman opened the door. She wasn't smiling.

"I'm Micah Wada."

"I'm Sarah Grimm. Come in," she said shortly.

Another woman, who Micah assumed must be Gail, waited in the living room, sitting on a large sofa. Sarah motioned Micah to a chair before sitting next to her sister. They looked like twins. Both in their late seventies. Both with white hair and wearing wire-rimmed glasses.

Micah told them a story he had repeated dozens of times during the campaign for the bond measure. He described the years of student overcrowding, and the fact that building new schools was the only way to resolve this crisis.

"We have a big challenge, though. It's been difficult to find vacant land."

"What would you build on our property?" Gail asked.

"An elementary school."

Sarah squirmed impatiently where she sat.

"We know about the overcrowding and the bond measure—how couldn't we? Every time we went to the mailbox, there was a brochure with propaganda about it. We must have been called half a dozen times by campaign volunteers—and always just as we were sitting down to supper."

She paused, glowering at him.

"We also know the School Board has the power to take our property. But you need to understand a few things. Our parents were the first farmers in this community. There was nothing here when they arrived. Nothing. They were part of a group of pioneers who founded this city."

"And they should never be forgotten," Gail said. "That's why you can't use the farm for a school."

"We plan to turn it into a history center and nature preserve," Sarah continued, "as a tribute to their bravery and perseverance."

Micah looked at each of the women. "I understand what you're saying. Sometimes, the past can be as important as the present."

And sometimes, he told himself, it's more important. Once these little old ladies come to a Board meeting and tell everyone how I intend to destroy a piece of the city's heritage, it'll be all over. I'll be told to find some other site—any site but this one.

"There's a way to use the school project to preserve the past," he said.

The sisters scrutinized him as he spoke.

"The property totals six acres. Usually, we'd need eight acres for a new school. If I can convince the city to let the children use Pearson Park during recesses and lunch, that will reduce the land we require—and allow us to save the house and barn. With funds from the State, we'll remodel them so they will be ready for exhibits and tours.

"And we'll call the school Grimm Farm Elementary."

The sisters glanced at one another.

"Where will the students come from?" Sarah didn't seem to be angry any longer.

"The neighborhood across the street."

The sisters looked at each other again.

"Mexicans will go to the school?" Gail said.

"Is that a problem?" he asked.

"It was Mexicans who helped our father harvest his lima beans." Sarah kept her eyes on him. "We're going to make sure their role is included in the history center's exhibits."

As the meeting ended, the sisters stood. He shook their hands.

"This is the start of a very special partnership," Micah said.

The old women smiled at him and nodded.

25

SEVEN.

Using State monies to rehabilitate the house and barn would have to be approved by officials in Sacramento. Despite his assurances to the Grimm sisters, Micah didn't expect this consent to come easily. In the past, these funds had never been used for anything except the construction of schools.

He booked a flight to the State Capitol and made an appointment to meet Solomon Sute.

Sute worked for Lee Grossman, a highly influential member of the State Senate. A retired structural engineer, Grossman had taken an obsessive interest in the construction and repair of public school buildings. This included creating rules which kept school boards from obtaining the State's financing. To Grossman, the rules guaranteed only the most deserving districts "crossed the finish line", as he liked to say, and received the monies they claimed to need.

Sute placed himself in the role of arbitrator when challenges arose regarding the meaning of his mentor's rules.

"We're not in the business of turning ramshackle farm buildings into museums," he growled.

"But my proposal will save the State money," Micah said. "Purchasing the Grimm Farm property, rehabilitating the old buildings and using Pearson Park as the school's playfield is less expensive than any other option."

Sute took the documents Micah had brought with him and studied them for several weeks. He had analysts within the State bureaucracy examine and verify the property appraisals and construction cost estimates. He even visited the district; he flew down from Sacramento one morning and Micah drove him around the city so he could see for himself that no other vacant land was available.

After the visit, Sute called Micah.

"I don't like your proposal," he said. "It could open the door to all kinds of strange interpretations of the rules. But I agree it's less expensive than the alternatives. So I'm going to allow it to be approved."

"I can't tell you how much I appreciate this—"

Micah stopped. Sute had hung up on him.

A few weeks later at the Capitol, the State Disbursement Board unanimously approved the Grimm Farm funding. At the end of the meeting, Micah crossed the crowded hearing room.

Sute stood in front of him. A large black man, standing over six and a half feet tall and weighing at least three hundred pounds, he glared down at Micah, who was offering his hand.

Sute shook it limply.

Micah continued to grasp his hand. "Have time for a drink?"

Sute studied him for a moment. Finally, he nodded.

They left the Capitol building and walked several blocks before stepping through the doorway of an anonymous-looking neighborhood bar. For the next two hours, the men shared a booth in the afternoon shadows, sipping glasses of bourbon on the rocks. Sute did most of the talking, regaling Micah with war stories about his years in State government.

As the shadows in the room lengthened, Micah glanced at his watch.

"I'd better grab a cab. My flight back to L.A. is taking off in an hour."

Neither of them was feeling any pain as they walked out into the Indian summer twilight.

"It was nice to talk with you," Micah said as they shook hands again.

"Same here," Sute boomed. He bent his huge body at the waist, until his face was in front of Micah's.

"You are a smart fucker," he whispered.

"I know."

They grinned at each other. Then Sute straightened up and began walking unsteadily down the sidewalk, back towards the Capitol building.

EIGHT.

During his drives around the community, Micah noticed a derelict motel in the city's downtown. In recent years, it had become a haven for drug dealing and prostitution. The police department was almost a daily presence on the property. The situation had deteriorated to the point that the motel's owner was only too glad to sell it to the district when Micah called him.

But as contractors prepared to break ground at Grimm Farm and the motel site, he struggled to move the construction program's most important project forward.

The district's two high schools had been constructed over thirty-five years before, when there was ample vacant land in the community. Each had originally been planned to educate fifteen hundred students.

The enrollment at each was now double that number.

On the new assistant superintendent's first day at the district, Dr. Hernandez urged him to visit the campuses. Micah spent several days at the schools.

What he saw shocked him.

Portable buildings were everywhere—even on the sites' front lawns.

At lunch, the students waited in line for a half hour or longer to pick up their food.

They waited in line at each school's attendance office.

They even waited in line to use the restrooms.

And the crush of bodies as the teenagers moved through the corridors between periods, trying to reach their next class before the bell rang, was overwhelming.

These schools reminded him of refugee camps he'd seen on the evening news. The overcrowding made him furious with those who allowed this to happen: the retired superintendent and the school board members of the past.

Unfortunately, land for the new high school would be the most difficult to obtain.

The campus would have three times the enrollment of an elementary school. In addition, it would have academic and arts programs with their own buildings, multiple playfields and gyms and a parking lot for the teenagers who were old enough to drive.

All this would require at least fifty acres, and possibly more.

An inventory of possible locations for the new school had been compiled by Micah and his consultants. It showed that the district would have to purchase numerous individual properties in order to create a site of sufficient size.

On the maps and aerial photos in Micah's office, these parcels were anonymous rectangles and squares. In reality, the exhibits represented the most important parts of people's lives: their businesses and their homes.

When they learned the district wanted their property, most of the owners would be outraged. And once they heard the news, the first thing they'd do is contact the Board members

And raise holy hell.

One afternoon, Micah was sitting at his desk, reviewing the property inventory, when his phone rang.

"Micah, Solomon Sute here."

A questioning look crossed his face. This was the last person he expected to hear from. "How are things in Sacramento?" he said.

"One hundred and ten degrees and the Legislature can't figure out how to pass a budget. Otherwise, everything's just fine!"

Both men snickered.

"Once the session ends," Sute said, "I'll be making a trip south. Let's get together while I'm down your way."

"Certainly," Micah agreed as he tried to guess the reason for Sute's visit.

They met at a bistro in an upscale mall on the city's east side. After they ordered their lunches, Sute leaned forward in his chair.

"Two years ago, Lee authored a piece of legislation called the land saver school law. Ever heard of it?"

Micah nodded. "It encourages districts without vacant land to try new ways to build schools."

"That's right."

Sute paused as the waitress arrived and placed salads in front of them.

"Eminent domain is a very pricey way to purchase real estate," he said after she left them. "Besides that, condemnation creates a lot of bad feelings towards school districts and the State.

"Instead of getting into expensive fights, Lee thinks districts and property owners should work together. His legislation has funding for a pilot project: a new school that can show other districts the benefits of cooperation."

Micah knew all of this, and more, about the land saver school legislation. He knew the pilot project would be handpicked by Grossman. And that Sute had been working with the state's largest and most overcrowded districts to try and move a project forward.

"I've heard there are already pilots in the works."

Sute frowned. "I've been trying for two years to get someone to use the legislation. So far, I haven't had any luck. And that hasn't made Lee happy."

"What about the school on top of a museum in downtown San Francisco?"

The State official shook his head as he picked at his salad. "Too hard to get all the parties to talk to each other."

"How about the school in the parking lot at Dodger Stadium?"

"Nope. The Dodgers vetoed the idea."

"And the school over the freeway in Santa Ana?"

Sute set down his fork and glared across the table.

"You been following me around?" he demanded gruffly.

Then he let out a boisterous laugh, causing several of the other diners to glance his way.

After he calmed down, Sute leaned forward again.

"You should be the one to build the pilot school. Your district has a tremendous need for new classrooms, but no vacant land. And I believe you could pull it off."

"I know I could," Micah said.

Sute brought two copies of Grossman's legislation with him. The men reviewed the bill's content as they ate their lunches.

Two provisions of the law stood out.

First, the State would pay the entire cost of the pilot project. There was no requirement for matching local monies, as was usually the case.

The second provision granted it priority over all other projects. The State facility program was not always funded, which meant a waiting list sometimes existed. The delay could be anywhere from a few months to several years.

The pilot project would jump to the front of the line.

These incentives were enormous. They meant a savings of tens of millions of dollars in local bond monies, since the land saver school would be paid for entirely by the State. And they meant the ability, as a result of the bill's priority language, to obtain State funding much more quickly than usual.

Micah walked Sute outside to his rental car. The big man tossed his sports coat into the back seat and turned to the assistant superintendent.

"There's one thing I want to make sure you understand. This project is Lee's baby. Every step of the way, he's going to want to be involved. He'll probably insist that you come to Sacramento to meet with him."

"That's fine with me."

When he returned to his office, Micah pulled out the property inventory and began flipping through its pages. He recalled that the largest parcel in the city was the site of an older shopping center called Fairview Plaza.

Here it is, he told himself, resting the open document on top of the desk's clutter. He leaned close and moved his finger under a line of data. The center was just under forty-five acres in size.

Micah had driven past it numerous times since coming to the district. Located at the intersection of two of the city's major streets, Fairview Boulevard and Raymond Avenue, the center included a collection of 1950's-era structures clustered in the middle of the property. To the north and south of these buildings were two large parking lots.

Several years ago, an additional freestanding structure had been constructed at the southeast corner of the site. The contrast between the older buildings—monolithic, off-white blocks—and the new one was striking. Arrayed in brilliant colors, it was architecturally vibrant, with varied roof lines and large windows.

Micah walked out to the BMW and made the short drive to the Plaza and the parking lot behind the original buildings. Acres of asphalt began at Raymond Avenue and swept across the site to the west property line, where a super market stood on the adjoining parcel. To the north was a narrow strip of landscaping and a six foot high masonry wall. Beyond the wall, he could see the rooftops and occasional second stories of the houses in the adjacent neighborhood.

Before he returned to his office, Micah turned the car north on Raymond Avenue. The houses closest to the Plaza were typical of the characterless dwellings real estate developers had built throughout Southern California.

As the boulevard continued northward, the neighborhood began to change. Now the houses were larger, mostly two stories in height, with sweeping front lawns. The architectural style of each varied, from Mission Revival to Art Moderne and English Tudor.

These were the homes of the city's elite, the doctors, lawyers and business owners; the residence of the community's congresswoman was located on one of the neighborhood's streets.

As soon as he got back to his desk, he dialed Judy's number.

"Have time to grab a cup of coffee?"

"Why…sure," she said.

The next day, they met at a Starbucks around the corner from city hall. After picking up their cups, the pair settled into a corner table.

"You're a busy man," Judy said. "It's been a long time since this city had two new schools under construction at the same time."

She was younger than he and petite, with the olive skin and high cheekbones of her Cocas ancestors. Her jet black hair was cut just above her slender shoulders.

Micah grinned at her.

"That's how I roll."

She smiled back at him. "And you do it well."

"I read in the newspaper that you've been busy, too," he said. "Handling Fairview Plaza's development application."

"Oh, yes. There's going to be some big changes. That center is in desperate need of a facelift. Have you seen the new building? They want to construct another at the opposite end of the Fairview frontage and remodel the older buildings to match the look of the new ones."

"According to the article, an outfit called New Design Enterprises owns the Plaza. I'd never heard of them before."

"I'm working with Sam Comstock, New Design's president."

She sipped her coffee. But she continued to study him.

"What else have you been up to?" she said.

"Trying to find some place to build the new high school. I need to ask: What does the city think of our construction program?"

"All five Council members supported the bond measure. And they love the Grimm Farm project. What a great idea—using a new school to preserve an important part of the city's history."

"I couldn't agree more," he said.

An amused look crossed her pretty face.

"What would the Council think if we built the high school in a shopping center?"

Her smile abruptly disappeared.

"I hope you're kidding."

"I'm facing a hell of a dilemma." The flirting had stopped. "Unless I can come up with a new way to create a site, the district will have to purchase a dozen or more contiguous parcels. I'd have to trust that the Board will stand up to the property owners and use its power of eminent domain."

"The city's leadership knows how overcrowded the high schools are," she said. "Believe me, we want to see that change. But Don would be beside himself if you tried to use a shopping center's property."

"Why would the city manager care?"

"Because of the lost sales tax revenue. The school will crowd out future stores. And the students' presence will scare away shoppers.

"Don told me your old district negotiated an agreement to use park land as school sites. Know why the city was so helpful? It was to keep you from going after real estate that generates sales taxes.

"He was concerned when he heard you were going to purchase the motel. Almost any other use would generate income for the city. But the motel was such a public nuisance that he decided not to stand in your way."

"Would Smith try and stop a school construction project he didn't like?"

She pressed her lips tightly together before answering.

"Yes, he would."

He gave her a sidelong glance.

"Too bad there aren't more parks in this city. And too bad the parks you have are so small."

She shook her head at his show of chutzpah.

"Have any lunch plans?" he asked.

She hesitated. "Not really."

"Where should we go?"

"Have you been to El Tapatio?" she said.

"No. Is it good?"

"It's been my family's favorite since I was a little girl."

They walked out to the street and Micah followed Judy's Toyota. At Raymond Avenue, she turned south, away from Fairview Plaza. On both sides of the wide road were the simple houses that young veterans purchased for their growing families after World War II. Long ago, most of these houses had been re-sold to the new arrivals from Mexico. Many of them were showing their age, and looked worn out.

Judy's brake lights blinked on and she turned right onto Main Street, a two lane thoroughfare bordered by multi-story brick buildings. Decades before, when the countryside was mostly occupied by farms, this street served as the town's main shopping district. After all these years—and despite the development of shopping centers such as the Plaza—it was still bustling; the sidewalks were filled with pedestrians.

At first glance, the snug streetscape and stone facades made the block seem a snapshot of small-town America straight out of a Frank Capra movie.

But the shop windows displayed Spanish-language signs.

Carnitas and tortillas were on sale at the butcher shops and markets.

The sporting goods stores featured the jerseys of Club America, Chivas and other Mexican soccer teams.

And the travel agencies advertised inexpensive flights to Guadalajara and Mexico City.

Judy braked the Toyota again and turned left, snaking into a gap in the stream of cars. Micah followed closely behind, squeezing through the same opening before the traffic could close up.

They soon entered a residential neighborhood. At the end of the street, Micah could see a neon pole sign. It proclaimed EL TAPATIO—BEST FOOD IN TOWN.

Judy pulled to the curb and Micah parked behind her. As he got out of his car, he realized the restaurant building had originally been a house. It seemed deserted. She led the way, walking up a short gravel path that crossed a patchy lawn. They stepped into a tiny lobby.

A woman in her sixties with twin braids of gray hair hanging down her back appeared from another room.

"Juanita!" she exclaimed with a smile, embracing the younger woman warmly. "It's been too long since I've seen you."

"I've been super busy at work."

She introduced Micah to the woman, whose name was Maria.

"He works for the school district," Judy said.

"Are you a teacher?"

"I manage the school construction program."

"You do!"

Maria grasped his right hand with both of her own.

"My grandchildren live down the street from Pearson Park. They are so happy about the new school!"

He grinned. "You just made my day," he told her.

The old house was divided into several small dining rooms, all empty of customers. Maria led the pair to a table in the back of the restaurant.

"She's a friend of my mother's," Judy said after the woman had left them.

"What does El Tapatio mean?"

"It's a nickname for natives of Guadalajara. My parents came from a village just outside the city."

"Were you born in Mexico?" he said.

"No. Right here. What about you?"

"I was born in L.A.—in the same hospital as my dad."

"That surprises me," she said. "When I first heard your name, I figured you must be from someplace far away. There aren't any other 'Micahs' or 'Wadas' around here."

"My grandfather was a Unitarian minister. It was his idea to name me after his favorite Old Testament prophet."

"What about 'Wada'?"

"It's the name of another figure from ancient times."

Judy looked perplexed. She was about to ask him to explain what he meant, but Maria reappeared with two menus.

When they were alone again, Micah set the menu down.

"You don't wear a wedding ring," he said.

"Neither do you. Have you ever been married?"

He didn't answer immediately.

"My wife had breast cancer. She passed away several years ago."

"I'm sorry. Do you have any children?"

He stiffened. "A son."

"How old is he?"

"Eighteen."

"Does he live with you?"

He leaned back in the chair and shook his head.

"Do you get to see him very often?"

"I haven't seen him since he was fourteen years old."

Suddenly, his voice sounded strangely flat and emotionless. It seemed to her that he had quickly grown very sad.

"That's a long time," she said.

Micah watched her for a moment before he spoke.

"He's a runaway."

A stunned expression crossed her face.

"Have you tried to find him?"

"Of course. I've contacted every law enforcement agency with a reason to help. For a while, I even retained a private investigator. But there hasn't been any sign of him. Not one clue I could follow up on."

He straightened himself then. "I'm hungry. What's good here?"

Judy didn't blame him for wanting to change the subject. She wished she could console him, except she didn't know what to say. At the same time, she wondered what had caused his son to run away. But she decided this wasn't the time to ask.

As they ate their lunches, he asked what she liked to do in her spare time. Soon, each knew the other's favorite TV shows, movies and songs. Both agreed that their favorite tune of the moment was a big radio hit from the previous year: Rod Stewart's version of "Reason To Believe".

"That line the narrator sings about being able to trust in the face of a lie—it's bittersweet, but it's also beautiful," he said.

She gave him a long, soulful look. "It's too bad, though, that one of them wasn't being honest."

"I'll tell you what song I can't wait to hear," he said. "'Welcome to the Monkey Bar!'"

Her face lit up, and she burst out laughing.

"I…can't…either!" she replied, between giggles.

When they were finished, Micah walked Judy to her car.

"I really enjoyed myself," he told her.

She smiled at him. "Let's do this again."

*   *   *

Late that afternoon, Micah switched off the lights in his office, stepped through the darkened bullpen (his staff had already left for the day) and out the glass door. He followed a concrete walkway to an adjacent building. The superintendent's office and the School Board's meeting room were located here.

Tonight, the room was being used by a group of community members who had been appointed by the Board to oversee the facility program and the use of the bond funds. For the next ninety minutes, Micah reviewed the district's construction activities and answered their questions.

When the meeting ended, he locked up the building, walked to the parking lot and drove to the nearby freeway.

His house was in an older neighborhood, part of the sprawl of anonymous development that had overwhelmed Southern California over the past fifty years. Micah and his wife purchased it when he was beginning his career in school facility planning. On the day they picked up the keys from the Realtor, the couple learned she was pregnant with their son.

The house was dark and silent. He walked through the living room and kitchen, switching on the television and several lights as he went.

There were two bedrooms. He went into the larger one and took off his suit and tie. Wearing a two-piece workout suit now, he walked to the refrigerator in the cramped kitchen and pulled out a can of beer. He took the beer into the living room and sat down in a large easy chair before the television. On the screen was an Angels baseball game.

Micah drank the rest of the six pack by the time the game was over. He shut off the television and the lights and walked down the short hallway to the master bedroom. After pulling off the workout suit, he shut off the light and slipped under the sheets.

This was the part of each day he dreaded.

In the mornings, he would be preoccupied with getting dressed and out the door. Once at work, he was overwhelmed with the demands of his job: providing direction to his staff and consultants; meeting with Dr. Hernandez and various community members; preparing for the Board's bi-weekly meetings; monitoring the projects.

In the evenings, there was the television and the beers—and sometimes, Scotch or bourbon.

But now, at bedtime, there were only he and his memories. Together in the bed he shared with his wife who was now gone. Down the hall from the bedroom of his missing son.

Sometimes, it seemed like the feelings of remorse and sorrow would overwhelm him.

This is when Micah reminded himself of how blessed he was to build schools. He thought of the children and teenagers who needed the classrooms he was creating. He ran through the roadblocks standing in the paths of the projects. Then he determined how to overcome them. He was supremely confident of his skill, and certain of the higher purpose that his career represented. This comforted him as he lay in the dark.

Tonight, though, he wasn't dwelling on his job. His solace came for a different reason. He was thinking of Judy. She was attractive and smart and fun to be with.

He told himself not to let his emotions get the best of him. After all, the reason she was so friendly could simply be because Don Smith wanted her to keep an eye on him.

Still, he couldn't wait to see her again.

NINE.

Later that week, Micah sat down with Dr. Hernandez and told him about the meeting with Solomon Sute.

"This is a great opportunity," the superintendent said.

"It could be. If we can find a site that satisfies Sute and Grossman—and is owned by someone who will agree to be our partner."

Micah noted that Fairview Plaza, as the largest parcel in the city, offered the best chance for implementing the shared use mandated by the land saver legislation. He described his visit to the center's north parking lot.

"But there may not be enough acreage for the school, even if we build up. Besides that, I have two concerns about parking.

"The shopping center has to comply with the city's standards. They prescribe a minimum number of spaces. When we construct our school, it'll wipe out quite a bit of the Plaza's parking. That could be reason enough for the property owner to refuse to sell us the land."

Dr. Hernandez cocked his head to one side. "Won't the city grant a parking variance to the center if that helps us build a new school?"

Micah explained the sales tax revenue issue—and the possibility that Smith might object to the project.

"That's not good," Dr. Hernandez said. "There's a reason why he's been the city manager for twenty-five years. He's a tough customer.

"What's the second concern you have about parking?"

"On a very small site, we'll have to figure out a way to provide parking for the students."

"Why not build a parking structure?" the superintendent said.

"Its footprint would use up a good deal of the property. We could construct a lot under the school's buildings. But if teenagers are parking their cars underground, it means they're out of sight."

Micah paused before going on. "A few months ago, a fifteen-year-old girl was raped in an underground parking lot at a New York City high school."

"I remember reading about that in the newspaper." Dr. Hernandez stared at him. "This is going to get complicated, isn't it?"

Micah nodded. "The sooner I meet with the Plaza's owner, the sooner we can start working through all these issues."

"Go ahead. And let me know what he says as soon as possible. The Board members are getting anxious to hear when we'll have a new high school."

TEN.

On the following Monday morning, Micah was sitting at his desk when the phone rang. It was Terry Rivers, the district's director of construction.

"I'm at the Grimm Farm project," Rivers said. "You'd better get out here."

As he drove to the site of the new elementary school, Micah wondered what could be wrong. The contractor had only moved onto the property the previous week.

There was a police car parked on the street when Micah arrived. He walked past it and around the contractor's job trailer, which was blocking his view of the site.

Rivers and the police officer were standing together on the opposite side of the trailer with the job superintendent and the building inspector. They formed a semi-circle beside a large yellow tractor. This was one of four pieces of heavy equipment, along with a grader, loader and excavator, which the contractor had delivered just before the start of the weekend.

The machine was covered with black streaks of graffiti. As he got closer, Micah saw that the tractor's engine had been vandalized. Someone had fired several shots into the engine block, and the top of the distributor and the spark plug wires were laying on the ground.

When Micah joined the other men, he realized the policeman was a young Latino.

"This is Officer Zavala," Rivers told his boss.

"They hit the rest of the equipment, too." Rivers nodded towards the three graffiti-covered machines at the far side of the property, next to the old farmhouse.

"Have any idea who did this?" Micah asked Zavala.

"It was the local gang. They left their calling cards every-where."

The policeman pointed to the sharp, angular stick letters that had been sprayed on the tractor.

"See this—WSC? It stands for the name of the gang, West Side Chicanos. And these letters, CG. They mean Chicano Gang."

Micah placed a finger on another graffito. "What about the number 13?"

"It's for the thirteenth letter of the alphabet, M. As in Mexican."

"Why would they do this—and on a school construction site, of all places?"

"To them, you're no different than a rival gang that's trespassing on their turf. As for this being a school project? Every single member of the gang is a dropout. Some of them didn't even finish eighth grade."

"You know quite a bit about them," Micah said.

Zavala pointed across Pearson Park to a row of modest dwellings.

"You see that little white house at the end of the street? My parents still live there. The gang members have been around as long as anyone can remember. My father told me they were here when he came from Mexico.

"They hung around my grammar school when I was a boy, and recruited some of the kids I grew up with: those without a father in the house, and the kids whose brothers were already in prison."

"Think they'll be back?" said Rivers.

The policeman put his hands on his hips and gazed past the tractor to the vandalized equipment in the distance.

"Probably not. But if I were you, I wouldn't take any chances. I'd have a security guard here at night."

ELEVEN.

Micah stood at the front entrance of the J.C. Penney department store, the largest building at Fairview Plaza. He was waiting for Sam Comstock. When he called New Design Enterprises' office that morning, he was transferred to Comstock's secretary and gave her his name.

"Just a moment," she replied.

"Comstock here. What can I do for you?"

Micah was startled by how quickly the businessman picked up his call. He introduced himself again and began to explain his role with the district.

"I know who you are," Comstock interrupted. "We contributed to the campaign for the bond measure. And I read about the Grimm Farm project in the newspaper. That was a clever idea."

The man spoke slowly, and in a friendly tone. "What's on your mind?" he said.

"You mentioned the Grimm Farm site. We're looking for other properties to use for school construction projects. I have an idea I wanted to share with you."

Comstock didn't hesitate. "What's your idea?"

Micah reviewed the land saver school legislation and the fact that "folks in Sacramento", as he put it, had asked the district to put together a pilot project.

"I'd like to build the school at Fairview Plaza," he said.

"What kind of school are you talking about?"

"A high school."

For the first time, Comstock paused.

"Has anyone ever done something like this before?"

"No."

That measured voice came on the line again. "How could we make this happen?"

"If you and I met at the center, it would be easier to figure it out."

"Sure. How about this afternoon?"

Around him, vehicles roamed the parking lot and patrons walked by to enter and exit the department store. The shopping center was a community crossroad of sorts. Jaguar sedans parked next to battered pick-up trucks, and young Latinas led their children past elderly white couples.

At that moment, he noticed a man walking steadily across the lot. He had a long face, short blonde hair and wore slacks and a dark sports coat but no tie. The man was headed directly towards Micah.

"Sam Comstock," he said, smiling broadly and extending his hand as he reached the curb.

"Interesting idea you have." He spoke deliberately, as he did on the phone. "Let me tell you about my company. We find older shopping centers that need some work. We go in, remodel the buildings, maybe construct some additional square footage, and sell the centers for a profit."

"Judy Gonzalez told me about your plans for the Plaza," Micah said.

"She's a nice gal, isn't she? I like working with her. Yup, we're going to turn this property around. We started with that building."

He nodded towards the new structure at the center's southeast corner.

"You see how attractive it is? Shoppers want the center to look interesting without being confusing. And they want to park close to where they're going to shop. If I didn't make it easy for them to walk from their cars to the stores, I'd take quite a haircut when I try to unload this place."

"A haircut?"

"That's right."

"What do you mean?" Micah said.

"The business school definition is taking a reduction in the stated value of an asset. My definition is giving someone a big discount you didn't want to give them."

He stared at Micah.

"Where were you thinking of building the high school?"

"There's only one place I saw that might have enough acreage."

"The rear parking lot?"

"You read my mind."

"Well, let's head back there."

44

Comstock led the way as they walked around the J.C. Penney building. The men stood side-by-side, staring at the acres of asphalt and its crisscross of painted spaces.

"What would this school look like?" Comstock said.

"There'd be several multi-story buildings. That's the only way we could create enough square footage on such a tight piece of property."

Comstock motioned towards the parking lot, where there was only a handful of vehicles. "The shoppers don't like parking back here. It's at the rear of the stores, and too far away. For me, it's wasted space."

He turned to Micah and smiled.

"I'd rather sell it to you."

Since his purchase of Fairview Plaza, the center hadn't generated the income Comstock expected. He needed additional cash flow to operate his company and finance the construction of the new building. Then he would sell the center and move on to his next project.

The timing of Micah's call couldn't have been more opportune.

"Do you think the city will cause you any problems if you lose all these spaces?" Micah said. "You may not meet their parking requirements anymore."

Comstock glanced at the ground.

"Good question."

He raised his head. "But I can figure that out pretty fast. Come by my office tomorrow afternoon."

TWELVE.

That evening, Micah steered the BMW up the driveway in front of his house and into the single-car garage. He walked back down to the curb, where a metal mailbox was mounted on a wooden post. As he stepped up the rise towards the front door, he casually flipped through that day's mail.

At first, there only seemed to be the usual advertising flyers and bills. Then Micah stopped. In his hand was a white business-size envelope who someone had addressed in large block letters. An imprint on the upper left corner read "Columbia Marina." The postmark was from Hammonton, Oregon.

For some reason, Micah felt an urge to find out what it contained as soon as he could. After unlocking the door, he sat at a small round table in the kitchen and impatiently ripped it open.

Inside was a single sheet of unlined white paper. At the top of the stationery was the marina's logo. The page was filled with the same simple block lettering as on the front of the envelope.

When his eyes fell on the note's first word, a chill went up his spine.

DAD—
HOPE THIS REACHES YOU. DON'T KNOW IF YOU STILL LIVE AT OUR OLD HOUSE. IT'S THE ONLY ADDRESS I HAVE. THE LAST 4 YEARS HAVE BEEN HARD. I WANT TO COME HOME. BUT I AM IN TROUBLE. HOPE I WILL SEE YOU AGAIN SOMEDAY SOON.
BENJAMIN

After re-reading the letter several times, he folded the paper and put it back in the torn envelope. Standing, he went to the garage, backed the car down the driveway and sped away from the house.

There was a public library a few minutes away. He circled the reception area until he found a bookcase full of atlases and the title he wanted: Northwest United States.

Pulling out the oversized, weighty book, he carried it to a nearby table. Still standing, he opened the atlas to the index of towns and cities. When he found Hammonton, he turned to the page the index listed.

Before him was a map showing the region where the Columbia River meets the Pacific Ocean. Flowing west from the interior, the river separated Washington and Oregon.

Micah had never visited this area and knew nothing about it. The presence of numerous bays, points and inlets caused him to assume the river's winding basin had originally been shaped by some massive and brutal geological force. These irregular shorelines conveyed the impression of a hard, unforgiving place— a feeling reinforced by the place names on the map.

Names such as Dismal Nitch and Cape Disappointment

The river met the ocean between a promontory along the Washington shoreline and a spit at the tip of a peninsula on the Oregon side. As his eyes followed the arc of the peninsula's eastern shore, Micah spotted the town of Hammonton.

When he returned to the house, Micah called information. Then he dialed the Hammonton Police Department's number and asked for the chief.

"I'm not sure if he's here." The receptionist, a young woman, spoke in a jittery, high-pitched voice.

"Can you find him? I'm calling from California."

"Ah, sure."

After a moment, a man's assertive tenor came on the line.

"Chief Petersen here."

"Chief, my name is Micah Wada."

He described Benjamin's disappearance four years before and the unexpected arrival of the note, postmarked from Hammonton and printed on the letterhead of the Columbia Marina.

"Tell me what he wrote."

After Micah read the words into the phone, Petersen said:

"I'm dealing with a situation that might involve your son."

Micah's grip on the receiver tightened.

"We're a small community. Everyone knows each other, so most people don't bother to lock things up. About a year and a half ago, folks started noticing that property was missing from their houses and vehicles and boats. At first, it was groceries and odd pieces of clothing. Then it got more serious. Cash and credit cards began to disappear.

"Last month, neighbors noticed lights on in a vacation house they knew should be vacant. We were able to get an officer out there. When he pushed open the front door, the intruder heard him and ran out the back and into the woods.

"My man got a good look at him, though. It was a young male, probably in his teens."

The policeman paused. "Does Benjamin know anything about sailing?"

"Sailing? You mean, as in operating a boat?"

"That's what I mean."

"As far as I know, he's never stepped foot on a boat in his life."

"After we almost caught the thief, he started stealing boats— including a twenty-two foot sailboat from the Columbia Marina. Sailing on the river is a way to stay one step ahead of us. But he's taking a huge chance."

When he heard this, Micah hunched forward.

"There's a series of sandbanks and shoals at the river's mouth called the Columbia Bar," Petersen continued. "It's one of the most treacherous stretches of water in the world. Sailors call it the graveyard of ships. Hundreds of freighters and other watercraft have sunk there over the years.

"Humongous waves appear out of nowhere when the river crashes into the ocean. Depending on the tide, conditions can change from calm to insane in a matter of minutes.

"Whoever is taking these boats doesn't understand how unforgiving the river can be."

At Petersen's request, Micah provided Benjamin's birth date, eye and hair color.

"Let me ask you something else. Why did he run away?"

The police chief heard Micah sigh.

"My wife had breast cancer. For almost a year, she went back and forth between the hospital and our home. At the same time, I was managing the construction of dozens of classrooms. I had to make sure they were all finished before the start of the next school year. Otherwise, hundreds of kids wouldn't have had any place to learn.

"Between taking care of my wife and doing my job, I didn't have much time for Benjamin." He cringed as he listened to himself.

"One afternoon when he and I returned from the hospital, he told me he was going out to see a friend. What he actually did was sneak behind a convenience store and set its trash bin on fire. The blaze spread to a nearby house, which almost burned down."

Micah hesitated. "Soon after that, my wife passed away. Then Benjamin started another fire. This time, it was at his school.

"A few months later, he got up before sunrise, taped a note on the windshield of my car and disappeared."

"What did he write in the note?"

"Negative things about me. The last line said something like 'You abandoned me a long time ago, so now I'm going to abandon you.'"

"You were nursing your wife and making a living for your family. It doesn't seem like he had any reason to be angry with you."

Micah didn't answer.

"If you accept what he thinks of you, you're being much too hard on yourself," Petersen said. "I've met a lot of bad parents. Believe me—you don't fill the bill."

This was not what Micah wanted to hear. He was sure he knew the truth: that Benjamin's disappearance, and all of the troubles the boy faced today, were a result of his neglect.

"You say he was a firestarter?"

"He started two fires that I know of," Micah said.

"There were probably others. They either didn't cause enough damage to be noticed, or they were blamed on someone else.

"I'll give you a call if something happens that you need to know about," the police chief told Micah.

THIRTEEN.

Sam Comstock's office was located on the new building's second floor. When Micah arrived, the real estate developer escorted him to a Spartan conference room. Spread on a long table was a site plan for the shopping center. The north parking lot had been overlaid with blue shading.

"That's the land I can sell to you," Comstock explained.

He pointed to a chart filled with notations and figures.

"I asked my traffic engineer to calculate how many parking spaces I have now, how many I'll need because of the future building and how many I'd lose because of the school."

Micah lowered his head and studied the analysis.

"Right now, we exceed the city's requirements," Comstock said. "But that changes when the new building's square footage is included in the calculation and the existing parking in the shaded area is removed."

"When that disappears, you'll be thirty spaces short," Micah said, reading the chart.

Comstock shrugged. "I'm not so sure that's a big deal. Everybody at the city keeps telling me they want to see the Plaza upgraded. If I insist I need the money from the school district to finance the improvements, I bet they'll grant me a parking variance."

Micah turned to him. "I asked Judy what the city would think of a school in a shopping center. I didn't tell her the center was yours, but I'm sure she figured that out. She said Don Smith would be dead set against it."

He repeated Judy's explanation of the revenue implications for the city.

"I don't see the harm in asking about the variance," Comstock said. He tugged at his shirt sleeve until he could see the face of his wristwatch. "It's almost time for me to knock off. Can I buy you a drink?"

They went down the stairs to a private lot where a silver Bentley was parked. Comstock drove the sedan to the same restaurant where Micah met Solomon Sute. At the front of the building, opposite the doorway to the dining area, a second entrance led to a small, darkened bar. The room was empty except for a white-haired man who was wiping down bottles of liquor.

While they settled onto a pair of stools, the bartender placed two coasters in front of them. Comstock ordered a gin martini.

"The same," Micah said.

When the bartender set the martinis in front of them, Micah raised his drink.

"To building our school."

The pair tapped their glasses together; then each took a sip of the cold, clear liquid.

"How will you figure out the value of my property?" Comstock said.

"I'll hire three appraisers, and each will calculate a purchase price, based on the property's highest and best use."

"Will they assume the highest and best use is as part of a shopping center?"

"They will."

"I've never heard of using so many appraisers," Comstock said.

"This project is going to be scrutinized by the State, the city, maybe even the newspapers." Micah watched him. "I need to demonstrate that the district acted responsibly—and be able to prove you didn't take us to the cleaners."

Comstock leaned towards his companion.

"You told me something like this has never been done before."

"So I did."

Comstock held up his glass.

"To making history."

*   *   *

The cabinet's weekly meeting took place on the morning after Micah visited Comstock. At its conclusion, Micah asked Dr. Hernandez if he was available for a few minutes. The old man nodded while the other assistant superintendents shuffled silently out of the room.

"Fairview Plaza's owner is interested in working with us," Micah said.

The superintendent bent forward in his chair.

"He and I took a look at the parking situation," Micah continued. "As I suspected, the shopping center will be out of compliance with the city's requirements. Comstock and I are going to meet with Smith and ask about a variance."

"You told me Don won't do anything to help us."

"But we need to ask the question. Then we'll know where we stand—and whether or not we have to come up with another way to solve the parking shortage."

FOURTEEN.

A week later, Micah's secretary sat down in the chair before his desk.

"The city manager's office just called about that meeting. I thought you'd want to know who's going to be there."

Micah raised his eyebrows. "Isn't it just Smith, Comstock and me?"

Keona looked down at her notepad. "There'll also be City Councilmember Betty Phelan and Ed Roth, the president of the North Raymond Avenue Community Association."

After the secretary left the room, Micah picked up the phone and called Comstock.

"Do you know the councilwoman and Roth?"

"Betty lives just north of Fairview Boulevard; she and Ed are two of the biggest supporters of the changes I want to make to the center."

"What's the community association?" Micah said.

"It was set up by the residents a while back as a social club to organize the neighborhood's annual Fourth of July barbecue. Since then, it's evolved into an advocacy group. A means to impact the Council's votes on issues the homeowners think might affect their part of town."

"Why would Smith invite Phelan and Roth to the meeting?"

"Why?" It sounded as though Comstock was surprised the question needed to be asked.

"For years, I've been telling them how great the center will be when I'm finished. Now they've heard you and I are going to build a high school in the middle of the place. They're probably mad as hell.

"If this meeting was between you, me and Smith, there might've been a chance to reach an accommodation. But the invitation to Betty and Ed means the city isn't interested in working with us."

Comstock paused. "You're not getting cold feet, are you?"

As he heard these words, Micah's fists clinched and his prominent forehead flushed crimson.

"Sam, we don't know each other very well," he said. "But take my word for it: This deal won't get killed because I got cold feet."

For a moment, there was silence on the line.

"I need to be sure you're still with me, partner," Comstock said.

Micah was angry, but he could set his emotions aside. All that mattered was maintaining the partnership with Comstock and getting the land saver funding.

"I'll be with you to hell and back," he said, "if that's what it takes to give the kids in this city a new high school."

FIFTEEN.

The city hall was the tallest building in the community. Constructed in the 1950's, during the city's original population boom, it towered over downtown; the only comparable structure was the county courthouse on the same block, completed fifteen years later.

Micah and Comstock met in the first floor lobby and stepped into one of the elevators. The city manager's suite was on the tenth floor, at the top of the building.

As they sat in the anteroom outside Smith's office, Micah's eyes scanned the wall behind the secretary's desk. It was filled with photos of every individual who had served as mayor since the city's incorporation. All men, all elderly and all white: It was as though the photos came from a family album of silver-haired siblings. Micah spied the picture of Myron Richland's father; he had served when the influx of new Latino residents began.

The office's door swung open and Don Smith stepped out. In his late fifties, the city manager had fair skin and a thinning head of blonde hair in the process of turning gray. His charcoal suit accentuated his tall, slender build. He sauntered over to the assistant superintendent and the two shook hands.

"Good to see you again," Smith noted easily. "Is Jim going to be here?"

"He's at a conference in Sacramento."

"That's probably for the best." He stared at the younger man. "Betty and Ed are pretty upset about your new school."

Before Micah could reply, Smith turned to Comstock and also pumped his hand.

"Judy tells me the plans for the center are almost ready."

Comstock smiled broadly. "That's right."

Smith led the pair into his office. In the center of the large room was a round conference table where Betty Phelan and Ed Roth sat. They rose from their chairs. Each greeted Comstock warmly. They shook hands with Micah, too, but without any sign of enthusiasm. He handed his business card to each of them and to Smith.

55

The councilwoman, who wore a dark business suit, was of medium height with short cropped brown hair. She served as the assistant general manager at the regional water district. Roth, the oldest person in the room, seemed underdressed for the meeting in a golf shirt and tan slacks. He owned the local Chevrolet dealership.

"I understand you want to talk with us about Fairview Plaza," Smith said, glancing at Micah and then Comstock.

Micah started to tell the story of the district's overcrowding crisis, but Phelan interrupted him.

"The Council unanimously endorsed the bond measure—we certainly know the issue. So please, don't waste our time with a history lesson." She sounded as though she was reprimanding a disobedient child.

"Then you know our most pressing need is for a new high school," Micah said. "It's been impossible to identify a vacant parcel with enough acreage. But the State has offered us a way to build the project."

He described the land saver school law, the benefits which its provisions would provide to the district and the plan to use the north parking lot as the school site.

Phelan stared at the shopping center developer.

"If you sell the north lot to them, how will the Plaza be able to meet the city's parking requirements?"

Comstock unrolled the site plan and reviewed the analysis.

"Since the number of spaces we're short is so small, I was hoping the city would grant me a variance," he said, glancing at the council member.

"That'd pave the way for the construction of the school," Roth said. "And we think the school is a very bad idea."

"Why is that?" Micah said.

Phelan spoke up again. "As you admit," she said, glaring at Comstock, "it will create a parking shortage at the Plaza. When shoppers can't find a space, they'll park in the neighborhood. And I don't think our residents want to see the streets in front of their houses turned into overflow parking lots for your center.

"But I'm even more concerned about the traffic. The intersection of Fairview Boulevard and Raymond Avenue is already the most congested in the city."

"When I drive south on Raymond in the morning," injected Roth, "the cars move at a crawl."

"I can only imagine what it would be like if hundreds of student drivers were trying to get to that intersection every morning," Phelan added, looking at Micah.

The assistant superintendent straightened himself. "I understand your concerns. I think they can be resolved as the project is designed."

"There's another big problem we haven't talked about," Roth said. "Sam's put together a wonderful plan. We're really excited about what's to come. But now…"

He stopped and looked at Comstock. "If this high school gets built, my neighbors and I aren't going to go near the place. It'll be like shopping on a high school campus. It'll ruin the center."

"Mr. Roth, I want to make sure you understand something." Comstock pointed to the shaded portion of the site plan. "This area is already isolated from the rest of the center. There are steps the district and I can take to make sure it stays that way after the school's constructed."

The older man suddenly grew animated. He dismissed Comstock's assurance with a wave of his hand.

"Hell, Sam. Once those kids are in the center, you know as well as I do they'll go wherever they want and do whatever they like. There'll be trash and graffiti all over our neighborhood. Nobody can prevent that." He glanced at Micah. "Not even the school district."

Roth turned back to Comstock. "Sam, why in God's name do you want to do this?"

"It makes good business sense for my company. The parking lot is wasted space. Hardly anyone parks there—regardless of what the code assumes. When I sell it, I'll use the proceeds to pay for the changes everyone wants."

Smith had been doodling on the back of Micah's business card. Now he raised his head.

"Sam, it sounds like you're determined to keep working with the district."

"Yes, sir. As I said, it makes sense for us. In fact, I may not be able to afford the improvements to the Plaza if I can't sell the parking lot."

"I don't think we'll be able to help with the parking variance. Our codes and regulations were put in place to ensure that we have a well-planned city. We need to make sure you play by the rules."

"I understand. And I'll be complying with all of the city's requirements."

Smith looked at Phelan. "Is there anything else we need to cover today?"

She glowered at Micah.

"You have no idea how upset the residents will be when they hear about this. You're making a very big mistake. And your Board members will pay the price for it."

As the two men stepped into the elevator, Comstock turned to Micah.

"Let's get a drink."

The bistro's shadow-filled bar was once again empty of customers. The same elderly bartender dropped two coasters before them on the mahogany surface. They said little until each had taken a sip from his martini.

"Shit!" Comstock hissed. He glanced at Micah. "We sure as hell need to keep the school separated from the Plaza."

He set down his glass, a look of bewilderment on his face. "How are we going to get around the parking issue?"

"I don't know yet."

"Have you hired an architect?"

"I'm meeting with her this afternoon."

"What's her name?"

"Ellen Vuong."

"Never heard of her."

"That doesn't surprise me," Micah said. "Most of her clients are school districts. Is it true your plans are almost finished?"

"Yup. Next week, I'll submit them to the city. When the timing's right, I'll amend my development application to include the school."

"We need to go to Sacramento and meet with Senator Grossman," Micah said. "It's important to show him we're moving forward with a pilot project."

"I'm ready whenever you are."

"I'll have Ellen put together conceptual plans, so we have something to review with him."

SIXTEEN.

Micah found Dr. Hernandez in his office, where the super-intendent's monthly meeting with the Parent Teacher Association representatives was just breaking up. The PTA leaders knew Micah from working with him during the campaign to pass the bond measure. As they filed out of the office, each of the women greeted him warmly.

Although Latinos made up the vast majority of the district's students, almost all of the PTA parents were Anglos. They represented the handful of elementary campuses, north of Fairview Plaza and east of the freeway, where most of the pupils were still white children. Once the Anglo students finished the sixth grade, their parents sent them to private intermediate and high schools outside the city.

Denise Evans, the last woman to emerge from Dr. Hernandez's office, smiled when she saw Micah. She was the president of the PTA chapter at Raymond Avenue Elementary, located a mile northeast of the Plaza.

In her mid-thirties, she had delicate, strikingly beautiful features and blonde hair that was styled in a pixie cut. The mother of three elementary school-age children, she had recently divorced her husband, the manager of a hedge fund and one of the most successful businessmen in the city.

"How are you?" The tone of her voice was pleasant and open.

"Just fine. Did you have a good meeting?"

"It's so impressive to hear about all the construction projects. You know, the contractor is about to start on the new multi-purpose building at our school." Denise hesitated. "It's too bad we can't get rid of all those portable classrooms cluttering up the playfield."

"I'm going to replace them with a new building, if I can find the money." Micah planned to pay for the addition with the surplus dollars he would have when the district received the land saver funds.

"You and Dr. Hernandez have been a godsend," she said.

He shook his head. "It's you and the other parents who convinced the voters to approve the bond measure. Every night when I visited the phone bank, I saw you there."

Denise set her blue eyes on him and smiled again.

After she left, he walked through the open doorway. Dr. Hernandez was sitting alone at a long table, scribbling on a pad of paper. When he looked up, the old man motioned for Micah to join him.

"Did you meet with Don?"

Micah nodded. "He wasn't the only one there."

"Oh?"

"Betty Phelan and Ed Roth also attended—at Smith's invitation."

The superintendent rubbed the knuckles of one hand across his chin. "I got to know both of them during the bond campaign."

Micah described Phelan's concern over the possibility of shoppers parking in the surrounding neighborhood because of a shortage of spaces at the Plaza.

"That means the city won't support a variance. They're also worried about increased traffic and students from the school loitering in the center.

"We'll do what we can to address the traffic issues in the project's design. And there are ways we can separate the campus from the shopping center. But I doubt that we'll be able to satisfy them."

"Why do you say that?"

"What they're really worried about is seeing brown kids near their mansions."

Dr. Hernandez pushed his thick lips together. "Then we're going to be in a fight, no matter what we do."

At that moment, the phone rang. The superintendent went to the desk and picked up the receiver. Even though Micah could hear only half of the call, that was enough to know the caller was Myron Richland. The Board president was doing most of the talking.

Finally, Dr. Hernandez spoke up. "If you remember, Myron, I'd told you Micah would be meeting with Don. For whatever reason, he invited Betty and Roth."

He listened for several more minutes before responding.

"That's an excellent idea. Yes, we'll be ready for the next Board meeting."

The superintendent replaced the receiver and returned to his seat at the conference table.

"Betty called Myron right after your meeting ended. She gave him an earful. All about how the high school students will overrun the shopping center and the neighborhood."

Dr. Hernandez paused. "That isn't all Betty said to Myron. She threatened to turn the voters against our facility program—and against any Board members who support the high school."

Micah stared at the old man. Many times at his previous districts, he'd encountered strident and emotional opposition to the projects he intended to build. But this level of invective by an elected official over a proposal to provide desperately needed classrooms was new to him.

For the first time, he grasped what he was up against.

"During closed session," the superintendent continued, "Myron wants us to review the reasons why we're looking at the Plaza. In the meantime, I'm calling the rest of the Board. The last thing we need is for Betty or one of the other Council members to blindside them."

SEVENTEEN.

Ellen Vuong owned the building where her firm was located. It stood on a drab street in an industrial area across the freeway from Anaheim Stadium. On the stark building's second floor was the architect's office. When Micah reached the top of the stairs, he stopped at the receptionist's station.

Before he had a chance to speak to the young man who was sitting before him, he saw Ellen. She was walking purposefully down a long hallway towards him, tall and slim in a snug purple dress. The woman's long black hair fell over her shoulders as she approached. Smiling broadly, she embraced him warmly.

"How did you know I was here?" he asked in mock amazement. "Have you added clairvoyance to all your other talents?"

Her penetrating eyes gleamed as she laughed.

"I hate to disappoint you. But it had nothing to do with any supernatural powers. I looked out my office window and there you were on the street, parking your red car!"

The woman spoke with a distinct accent. Her vowels sounded long and lazy, and her words rose and fell in a lilt.

Ellen's family fled Vietnam after Saigon fell to the Communist forces. Upon arrival in Houston, the Vuongs were assigned to live temporarily in a city of tents that had been erected at Fort Chaffee, a military base in northwest Arkansas. The family moved into their tent two weeks before Ellen's sixteenth birthday.

After three months, the Vuongs were sponsored by the congregation of a nearby Southern Baptist church. The church members found the family an apartment, helped Mr. Vuong get a job and taught Ellen and her younger sister how to speak English. Most of this instruction was conducted by a retired school teacher who had spent most of her life in the Boston Mountains. As a result, Ellen spoke her second language with a hillbilly drawl.

She led Micah past the receptionist's station to a large table made of plywood. Several plastic chairs set haphazardly around it. She took a seat while Micah unrolled the Fairview Plaza plan.

"So, we need to prepare a site plan for the high school," she said while she studied the drawing.

"And it needs to include a parking lot with thirty spaces for the shopping center."

She looked up.

"I don't know if you have enough acreage for the extra spaces. Especially considering the amount of parking the school will require. What are you planning its enrollment to be?"

"Two thousand students."

"I'll be honest with you. This site presents quite a challenge. We should have fifty acres. Instead, we've got less than twenty-five percent of that."

She paused.

"You really are expecting me to be a magician!"

"We may both have to pull a few rabbits out of our hats before we're through," he said. "Except I don't own one."

"A rabbit or a hat?"

"Neither!"

"That's all right. I'll loan you one of mine."

"Which one?" he said.

She let out a giggle.

"Oh, stop it!"

EIGHTEEN.

Under State law, the School Board was allowed to meet in closed session to review ongoing negotiations and pending litigation. The meeting was held in a conference room next to the auditorium where the Board would convene later that evening for its public session.

Dr. Hernandez and Micah sat next to each other at a huge rectangular table, awaiting the arrival of the Board members. The superintendent leaned sideways so his face was close to that of the younger man.

"I've talked to each Board member," he confided. "And Betty's talked to each of them, too."

"What did they say about the project?"

"Not much—other than repeating all the bad things Betty told them." Dr. Hernandez raised his head and glanced at the clock, mounted on the opposite wall. It was almost time for the closed session to begin.

At that moment, the Board members began to file into the room. Myron Richland, Phil Putnam and Connie Carr were the first to arrive.

Richland managed one of the departments of the county government. Initially elected when he was only twenty-five years old, he had served on the Board for over ten years.

Putnam, a vice president at the regional office of a large insurance company, founded the city's first youth soccer league when his children were in elementary school. Twenty years after his days as a college player, the man was still trim of frame.

Tall, with ivory skin and a full head of curly red hair, Carr owned a modest dress shop and was a former president of the district's PTA chapter. She was married to a chemistry instructor at the local community college.

As the trio settled into their chairs, the last two Board members walked into the room.

During her campaign, Violet Yeoman called herself a full-time mother. In fact, she worked as an administrator at the Christian school that her five children attended. The woman, who was overweight and favored gray and navy blue business suits, had run unsuccessfully for a seat in the U.S. Congress after her election to the Board.

The previous year, an initiative was placed before the state's voters that would have made it legal for parents to pay the tuition at private schools, including those with a religious affiliation, using taxpayer funds. This money would be taken from the State budget, reducing the resources for public schools. Yeoman served as the Southern California campaign director for the measure, which was soundly defeated.

Jon Laird, the Board's newest member, attended the same church as Yeoman and had also been a vocal supporter of the private school initiative. Micah was not sure how the short, rotund man made a living. During his campaign, Laird claimed he was a real estate developer, but he never seemed to develop anything.

Richland called the closed session to order.

"Jim has talked with each of us about constructing the new high school at Fairview Plaza," he said. "I've asked him and Micah to review the project's status."

"This school will affect a lot of people's lives," Laird interrupted impatiently. "Why are we discussing something this important behind closed doors?"

"Jon, we don't want the property owner to know what we think about the parcel's suitability or value," Dr. Hernandez said. "That could impact the negotiations over the price. Second, there are individuals who oppose the school. If they decide to file a lawsuit, we must be able to review our legal strategy among ourselves."

Yeoman spoke up. "We haven't decided if we want to purchase this property. And no one has filed a lawsuit, or even threatened to file one." Her voice was high-pitched and strident. "We shouldn't be talking about this school in private. Not yet, anyway."

"I promise that Jim and I will check with our legal counsel to be sure this is appropriate for closed session," Richland said. "In the meantime, our staff is prepared to provide us with information about the project tonight."

He watched Smith and Laird for several seconds. When they didn't object, he turned to Dr. Hernandez and Micah.

"Go ahead."

Micah rose and spread a copy of the Fairview Plaza site plan on the table. The Board members leaned forward while he pointed out the shaded area, overlaid over the north parking lot, where the school would be built.

After giving the plan a perfunctory glance, Yeoman spoke again.

"Betty Phelan lives in that neighborhood. She tells me the school is a catastrophe waiting to happen. The traffic will be a nightmare, with hundreds and hundreds of teenagers trying to get to the intersection of Fairview and Raymond every morning."

"I met with Ms. Phelan last week," said Micah, who was still standing, "and explained that the traffic issues will be addressed during the design of the project." He glanced at the faces around the table. "Right after the bond measure passed, you approved a list of architects to design our projects. One of these firms is Vuong Architects. I've asked Ellen Vuong to prepare conceptual plans for the new high school."

Phil Putnam raised his hand. "Where do we go from here?"

"I'll be meeting soon with Senator Grossman, the author of the land saver legislation," Micah said. "His support of our project is crucial."

"This is an exceptional opportunity," Richland said, looking at his peers. "I think it's essential that our staff continue to pursue it."

Putnam and Carr nodded.

"Violet," Richland said, "I assume you won't object if our architect addresses Betty's concerns."

She glared at Micah with her beady eyes.

"There must be better places to build a high school—places that don't turn people's lives upside down."

"I don't agree." Richland was beginning to sound testy. "In a built-out city, a high school is going to inconvenience someone, regardless of where we build it. I think our staff has brought us the best possible option."

Frowning sullenly, Yeoman didn't respond.

*   *   *

Before the public session began, Connie Carr pulled Micah aside. They huddled in a narrow hallway at the rear of the meeting room.

"Betty's opposition scares me," she admitted lowly as they stood face-to-face. She was only an inch or two shorter than him.

"My term ends next year, you know. She called me this morning and said she'd find someone to run against me if I support the high school."

Connie stared at him. "I want to do the right thing. But I need your help. I don't really know much about the project. Or construction in general, for that matter. Do you think we could get together so I can pick your brain?"

Since he'd joined the district, they hadn't said more than a few words to one another. He hadn't paid much attention to her until now. As he gazed into her deep green eyes, it struck him that she was quite attractive.

"Sure," he told her. "I'll be glad to help you."

NINETEEN.

A few minutes before the start of the Board's next meeting, Micah was walking from his office to the auditorium when he noticed Betty Phelan and Violet Yeoman, standing next to each other at the far edge of the parking lot, engaged in an animated conversation.

Part of each meeting was set aside for comments from the public. When Richland, as the Board president, asked if anyone in the audience wished to speak, Phelan rose from her chair near the front of the room and stalked to the podium. It was positioned directly before the dais where the Board members and Dr. Hernandez sat.

"I know what a difficult job you have," she began. "State funding for education programs is not adequate. And the overcrowding of our schools is a challenge that has existed for many years. That's why I and the rest of the Council supported the bond measure.

"I understand the great need we have for more classrooms. However, I've learned about an idea your staff is pursuing for a new school that makes absolutely no sense."

She met the eyes of each Board member.

"They want to build a high school in the parking lot at Fairview Plaza," she announced.

Many in the audience gasped audibly when they heard this. It was the first time the public had learned of the project—and its location.

"Board members, this school would be a disaster for the homeowners near the shopping center," the councilwoman warned ominously. "It would mean unbelievable congestion at Raymond and Fairview. It would mean gridlock for those trying to travel on Raymond Avenue. And the adjacent residential streets would be turned into parking lots for the high school students."

She firmly grasped each side of the podium.

"I and many others believe there are much better locations for the new school. We want to work with your staff to investigate these sites."

Before she could continue, Richland spoke up.

"This subject is not on the meeting agenda. As an elected official, I'm sure you know what that means. State law prevents us from responding to your comments."

Phelan didn't look pleased.

"Very well," she snapped. "But you'll be hearing much more in the days ahead from me and the rest of the community."

She turned and, while the audience members gaped, stomped away from the podium and out of the meeting room.

Out of the corner of his eye, Micah saw a silhouette take the empty chair next to him. He turned to face Kent Hamish, a reporter from the local newspaper. The men had talked many times since he arrived in the city, especially during the campaign for the bond measure and when the agreement with the Ross sisters to build the new elementary school was announced.

Hamish leaned close to Micah.

"Have a few minutes?" he said lowly.

Wordlessly rising in unison from their seats, the pair walked through the meeting room's double doors and out to the parking lot. They stopped under a pole light which emitted an eerie yellow glow.

"Does the district plan to build a high school at the Plaza?" As he spoke, the reporter pulled a small notebook from the back pocket of his trousers.

"It's one of the sites we're studying. That's all I can say."

The slight man began to scribble on the notebook's page. "But a high school at a shopping center; that's pretty unusual, isn't it?"

Micah didn't answer.

"Would this be the first high school of its kind in the state?"

Micah frowned. The last thing he wanted the residents north of Fairview Plaza to read was that the district planned to construct an untried experiment in their neighborhood—even though that was exactly what he intended to do.

"I don't know," he lied.

"The councilwoman claims she's concerned about parking and traffic. Should she be worried?"

"We've just started looking into the site. It's too early for me to know what the traffic impacts will be. But regardless of where we build the high school, we'll work closely with the community during the planning process."

Hamish stopped writing.

"This is going to be a big story — the biggest this community's seen in a long time. Maybe the biggest ever. Not only because it's a one-of-a-kind project, but because a councilmember is opposed to it."

He sounded excited by the prospect of covering the brewing controversy.

"I have to get back to the meeting," Micah said. "Do you have any more questions?"

"Not tonight."

TWENTY.

Connie suggested that they rendezvous after the Board meeting at a bar in an adjacent city. It was part of a recently constructed complex that included a high-end restaurant and luxury hotel. Micah arrived first and waited outside until she pulled into the lot and parked her Dodge Dart.

She led the way into the building; it was apparent that she had been here before. He followed her through the hotel lobby to the bar and a booth that was tucked off by itself in a corner, screened from view behind a hedge of garishly green plastic palm bushes.

"Betty was sure full of herself tonight," she said, sounding exasperated.

"She and Violet were in the parking lot before the meeting began, huddled together like conspirators."

Connie shook her head. "What a pair."

"It's a good thing you, Myron and Phil are on the Board. Otherwise, I doubt that we'd be building a new high school."

She stared at him. "Is it true there's no place else where we could put it besides Fairview Plaza?"

He nodded, and told her about the city-wide property inventory and the criteria Lee Grossman had imposed in order to receive the land saver funding.

"I hope we can get the Board's approval of the project behind us before my re-election campaign starts," she said.

"In the meantime, I'll do all that I can to protect you," he promised.

She looked into his eyes.

"I appreciate that. Very much."

When the server came by, they ordered Manhattans.

"It's strange how things turn out," she said after taking a sip of the cocktail. "Betty's a district parent. She has a son and daughter at Raymond Avenue Elementary. When I was the PTA president, we were good friends."

"How long did you lead the PTA?"

"Five years. That's why I ran for the Board. As I became more involved with the district, I realized we needed a change in leadership if we were going to solve our biggest problems."

"Such as the school overcrowding?"

"Exactly." She paused. "Violet didn't want to hire you. She claimed your position wasn't necessary."

"I'm glad you disagreed."

"We'd be up the proverbial creek without a paddle if you hadn't come along."

"Coming from you," he said, "that means a lot to me."

She kept her eyes on him as she picked up her drink and took a sip.

"Dr. Hernandez told me you have your own business."

"Yes. A dress shop."

"Between managing your shop and dealing with your Board responsibilities, you must be very busy."

"My only child, Jeffrey, went off to Harvard last fall. So now it's just my husband and I at home.

"Thank God I have my outside interests."

She sighed. "Richard's much older than I am. As the years pass, there's less we have in common. Being parents was the one part of our lives we still shared. With Jeffrey out of the house, I feel like I'm living with a stranger."

"I'm lonely, too," he said. "I'm a widower, you know."

They stared silently at one another for a moment.

Reaching across the table's top, he took her hand. As he squeezed it, he could feel the edge of her thumb, rubbing at the inside of his palm.

"Get us a room," she said.

Wordlessly, he stood and walked back to the hotel lobby. When he returned, he set a key before her.

"We're on the fifth floor. Room five-oh-three," he told her. "I'll meet you there in fifteen minutes."

He went into the lobby again, picked up a newspaper from a stack on the registration desk and lowered himself into an easy chair. After glancing through most of the paper, he set it aside and took an elevator car to the fifth floor.

Once he closed the door to Room 503 behind him, he was engulfed in darkness. As he stepped forward, he inadvertently kicked an unseen object, sending it skipping across the room's carpeted floor.

"Hey! Be careful!" Connie whispered. "That's a new pair of shoes!"

Micah quickly stripped, dropping his clothes in a pile at his feet.

"I'm waiting," she said softly.

He took several steps forward.

"Am I getting close?"

"You're warm."

"And thinking about you is making me hot!"

She giggled.

Another step and his shin bumped against the bed's metal frame. He stretched his arm down through the blackness until the tips of his fingers found her bare, flat stomach. Kneeling beside the bed, he cradled her face in both of his hands. They kissed passionately. Then he slipped in beside her.

When she thought they had finished their lovemaking, she turned on a reading lamp at the side of the bed. While he watched, she raised her arm to study her wristwatch.

"I'd better go," she said, turning her face to him.

"Not yet. We're not through."

"Is that right?"

"That's right," he replied, reaching over her freckled shoulder to switch off the light.

TWENTY-ONE.

When Ellen arrived, Micah led her from his cramped and disorderly office to a conference room on the opposite side of the bullpen. Two small tables had been pushed together to create a larger work surface. While he stood beside the architect, she opened a long, red leather carrying case, pulled out an oversized sheet of paper and unrolled it.

The site plan for the new high school, it showed the outlines of a pair of two story buildings. One had a much longer footprint than the other. These adjacent rectangular structures formed an 'L'.

Ellen pointed to a parking lot that filled the land between the smaller structure and Raymond Avenue.

"This is for the staff and visitors."

He looked at her.

"Where's the rest of the parking?"

"We could turn the playfields into a second parking lot, or build a garage under the school buildings," she said. "Because there's so little acreage, though, putting more parking on our property creates an insurmountable problem.

"Once on the campus, there won't be enough stacking area for the cars as they wait for a space. They'll back out onto Raymond Avenue."

And Betty Phelan's prediction of a traffic nightmare will come true, he thought.

"There's enough stacking area for staff and visitors," Ellen said. "And for the cars dropping students off at the school's entrance. Traffic-wise, this site can work if there's no student parking. Or spaces for the shoppers."

She paused. "But that's only because I waved my magic wand and reduced the school's capacity from two thousand to twelve hundred students."

Micah grasped the back of a chair, pulled it from the table and took a seat. Ellen sat across from him. He placed an elbow on the table top and rested his chin on his fist.

"What'll we do about parking for the students and the Plaza?" she asked.

He raised his head.

"What does your crystal ball say?"

"I left it at my office."

"Some consultant!" He gave her a mischievous look.

"There's only one thing to do. It's time for a seance."

"A what?"

He leaned forward, closed his eyes and pressed his fingertips against each side of his temple.

"Planning spirits," he intoned, slowly and solemnly, as Ellen began to titter. "How can we create parking for these students?"

Puckering his lips, he squeezed his eyes shut so tightly that crow's feet appeared at their corners.

"Everything's foggy…

"Wait. I'm beginning to make out the spirits' answer.

"Yes, it's become clear. I can see six words.

"Here is what they say:

"'That is a damn good question.'"

Ellen laughed and pushed playfully at his shoulder. "Those spirits are no help at all!" she cried.

"You're telling me! I'm gonna fire their asses and bring on new ones—as quick as I can."

TWENTY-TWO.

Early the next morning, Micah met the superintendent at his office. The men were traveling together to a conference in San Diego. They drove away in the old man's Mercedes sedan, stopped at a Starbucks for coffees and pulled onto the freeway's southbound lanes.

Because of the hour of the day, there was little traffic congestion. But that would change after they passed through Camp Pendelton and joined the mass of vehicles which were headed for downtown San Diego at rush hour.

"I met with Ellen Vuong yesterday," Micah said as Dr. Hernandez set the car's cruise control.

He watched the old man. "I told you the Plaza site might not be large enough for the project. Her plan shows it's too small for a school of two thousand students."

The superintendent turned to him.

"How many can it serve?"

"Twelve hundred."

Micah shifted in his seat. "The lack of land impacts the school's design in another way. There isn't enough room for a student parking lot."

Dr. Hernandez was holding his cup of coffee. When he heard this, he was so surprised that he almost dropped the cup.

"No student parking at all?" he asked impatiently, glaring at the younger man.

"The site can't handle the vehicles waiting for a parking space. They'll stack up onto Raymond Avenue. Every morning, it would be chaos."

"I hope you've figured out where the students are going to park," Dr. Hernandez said.

"Raymond Avenue Elementary's campus is less than a mile away," Micah said. "The State will probably let us use part of the land saver funding to replace the portables there with a new classroom building. This will free up enough acreage for us to build the high school's parking lot on part of the playfield."

"And how will the students get from the elementary school to Fairview Plaza?"

"It's a short walk."

"Do you really think a teenager with a car will walk almost a mile to get to school?" The old man sounded incredulous.

"The district may need to provide shuttle vans," Micah admitted.

"Teenagers aren't going to like waiting for a van any more than they'll like walking to the school." The superintendent glanced at him again. "We have to give Betty and her neighbors an ironclad guarantee that the students will park where they're supposed to."

"What if the Board designated the land saver campus as a special school?" Micah said. "A school with higher standards, including a strict code of conduct? The code could prohibit parking on the neighboring streets and in the Plaza. It could even ban loitering in the shopping center and the surrounding neighborhood."

A smaller student body.

Higher standards.

More discipline.

Those are the traits of the state's most successful high schools, Dr. Hernandez told himself. Schools with outstanding test scores and high graduation rates. Schools whose graduates go on to the best universities.

The superintendent adjusted his grip on the steering wheel. This coin had another side, though. Not only was the high school going to be in a shopping center; it would be governed by rules and standards that hadn't even been established yet.

And its parking lot would be nearly a mile away at an elementary school.

"We're playing a high-stakes game," he said aloud. "We may create one of the best high schools in the region, a school that'll truly meet the needs of our students.

"Or you and I may fall flat on our faces in front of the Board and everyone else."

"We don't have a choice," Micah said. "We have to build this school."

Ahead of them, the traffic was beginning to slow. A series of beach towns lined the freeway's path as it wound south along the shore of the Pacific Ocean. At each onramp, more vehicles pulled onto the freeway. Soon, it was so congested that the traffic was barely moving forward.

"We need to do something else—convince the public that this project is a necessity. That it's the linchpin of our plan to end the overcrowding," Micah said.

"I like that," Dr. Hernandez replied. "We've got to stand up for the Board members. If we don't defend them, Betty and her allies will turn them into punching bags."

As the superintendent spoke, Micah continued to watch him. He had his own reason for proposing this campaign of outreach to the community. The more support that developed and grew within the city for the new school, the more pressure the Board would feel to build the campus—despite the opposition of Phelan and the residents north of Fairview Plaza.

She wanted Connie and the other Board members to believe their political futures were in peril if they pushed for the high school. They needed to see there would be a political price to pay if they DIDN'T build the project.

When San Diego Harbor came into view, the old man turned the Mercedes down an offramp and steered it through the crowded downtown streets until they reached the valet parking lane of a large hotel.

As they walked into the lobby, Solomon Sute stepped in front of the pair.

"Good to see you, man!" he said loudly, grasping Micah's hand with his own and shaking it vigorously.

After Micah introduced Sute to Dr. Hernandez, the big man glanced down at each of them.

"Lee's looking forward to meeting with the district."

"I understand the senator is speaking this morning," Micah said.

"That's right." Sute turned to the superintendent. "Lee's been coming to this conference for years. School construction is his passion."

"Our Board certainly feels honored to use his legislation," Dr. Hernandez said.

When he heard this, a smile of satisfaction crossed Sute's face.

Behind him stood a stocky figure with a thick shock of black hair. Micah noticed he was cocking his ear in the direction of the trio, as though trying to overhear their conversation. When the men's eyes met, the stocky man turned and walked away.

The conference was sponsored by an organization that lobbied the governor and members of the State Legislature on behalf of school districts like Micah's with desperate facility needs. He had served on the organization's board of directors for many years. As he and Dr. Hernandez made their way through a hallway to the hotel's ballroom, the assistant superintendent was greeted by a constant stream of well-wishers.

"Is there anyone here who doesn't know you?" Dr. Hernandez asked loudly over the din in the crowded passageway.

"Only if they've been living under a rock," Micah said while he shook another hand.

By the time the conference was gaveled to order, over five hundred attendees were seated at large round tables spread across the ballroom's floor. The pair sat at the rear of the huge room. Micah could see Sute at the front of the chamber, just to the side of the stage.

The organization's chairperson, a middle-aged woman who managed the facility program at a school district outside of Fresno, stood at the podium. She announced that the conference's opening speaker was a special guest and close friend.

"Senator Lee Grossman has been a supporter of public school facilities since he was elected thirty years ago," the chairperson explained. "He has always been there for us when we needed him."

She proceeded to highlight his accomplishments, including authorship of the legislation that created the Lee Grossman State School Facility Funding Program.

"We need this man more than ever," she proclaimed. "Please join me in welcoming back to our conference Senator Grossman."

As the audience applauded enthusiastically, a tiny figure rose from a chair next to Sute and moved slowly to the steps that led to the stage. He wore thick eyeglasses and had a full head of wavy white hair.

After gingerly navigating the steps and shaking hands with the chairperson, the senator shuffled past her to the podium. He pushed his glasses further up on the bridge of his large nose as he stared at the audience. His head was the only part of his body visible to the attendees.

"Coming before you today reminds me of the man who visited his doctor for his annual physical exam," Grossman began. He had been born and raised in Brooklyn and spoke with the accent of his birthplace.

"At the end of the exam, the man's doctor asked: 'What do you want first—the bad news or the bad news?'"

The audience members laughed politely.

"Well, I've got some bad news for you, and some more bad news."

Micah had heard this speech—or, rather, various versions of it—many times over the years. The joke might be different, and the bad news would vary in its specifics. But the speech's core always included the same two messages.

One, the other politicians in Sacramento, including the governor, didn't understand or care about the need for school facility funds.

And two, Grossman would somehow bring the rest of the politicians to their senses.

The senator told the audience he had introduced a bill to place a billion dollar bond on the next general election ballot.

"That's right. I said a billion. As in a number with nine zeroes."

Micah listened to him describe the upcoming battles that must be fought and won. "This legislation still must be approved by policy and fiscal committees, not only in the Senate, but also in the Assembly. And then the governor—who, I don't need to remind you, has never been a friend of bond measures—must be convinced to sign the bill."

There were thirty-nine other senators and eighty assembly members in the California Legislature. Not one of them saw school facilities as their number one priority. Grossman did—and because he was a skilled and very senior senator, the old man had always been able to convince the rest of the state's leadership to support his bonds.

"We have our work cut out for us," Grossman said. "But we've fought these battles before. And we've always been successful. So, who knows. Maybe the patient will live through the surgery."

The rest of the morning was devoted to presentations by the organization's lobbyists and a spokesperson from the State Disbursement Board. As its chief of staff, Sute usually represented the Board on such occasions. Today, though, he did not take the stage. Instead, the stocky man who Micah saw earlier stepped to the podium.

"Hello, everyone." He spoke through a buzz of feedback as he pulled at the microphone.

"I haven't had a chance to meet most of you yet. My name is Fred Foster. The governor recently appointed me to manage the Board's real estate division. We're the ones who stop you from getting yourselves or the State in trouble."

Although Foster smirked as he said this, the audience didn't think his comment was funny.

"The State disburses hundreds of millions of dollars for real estate acquisitions. It's my division's duty to insure you're not throwing that money away," he said while the murmuring continued in the crowd.

"What's even more important is guaranteeing the land you buy is free of contamination. Let me put it to you this way: The safety of our children and their teachers is our number one priority."

He grinned again as he looked down from the stage.

"As long as you act responsibly, you and I will get along fine."

There was scant applause—but plenty of grumbling—as Foster stepped down.

At noon, the hotel staff wheeled several large tables filled with bowls of salad and platters of sandwiches into the ballroom. While the chairperson adjourned the morning session, Dr. Hernandez and Micah joined the rest of the attendees in the buffet line.

Micah had just picked up a plate when he felt a hand on his shoulder. Sute was standing next to him.

"Lee and one of his aides had to get back to Sacramento, so there's space at my table. Would you and the superintendent like to join me?"

After the three men settled into their chairs, Micah turned to Sute.

"Who's Fred Foster?"

Frowning, the big man set down his fork.

"He's a donor to political campaigns. The governor feels the State can't afford any more bond debt. As you heard this morning, Lee doesn't agree. So, the governor decided to teach my boss a lesson and sent Foster to the Disbursement Board.

"Ever since he got there, the bastard's raised holy hell. Last week, he marched into my office with a file for a new elementary school. 'Look at what the district paid for this school site!' he screamed. I took the file, found the property appraisal and showed him they paid exactly what the appraiser estimated the property was worth.

"You know what he did then? He ripped the appraisal out of my hand and threw it across the room.

"'I've been buying and selling real estate for twenty years,' he shouted. 'And they paid too goddamn much!'"

Sute continued to stare at Micah.

"The son-of-a-bitch is out of control."

TWENTY-THREE.

Since their initial tryst, Micah and Connie had been going to the hotel after every Board meeting.

"My husband is beginning to wonder why the meetings are lasting so long," she said as they lay naked next to one another.

"Tell him it's the fault of that facility planner and his high school project."

"He knows about the project. Everyone does. But I don't want him to know you exist. He's very jealous."

"How jealous?"

"He's accused me of having affairs with men I've never even met!"

She slipped out of the bed and switched on a floor lamp so she could see to put on her clothes.

"What's that?"

He pointed at one of her bare thighs. Near the top of her leg was a patch of crimson flesh.

"I don't know. It appeared a few weeks ago. At first, it was about the diameter of a dime. But it keeps getting bigger." She rubbed at it gingerly with her fingers. The rash was as large as her hand.

"Does it hurt?"

"It didn't at first. But in the last week or so, it's become painful to the touch." She raised her head. "That's why I wanted to be on top tonight."

"I've never seen anything like that. You should visit a doctor."

"I think I'd better."

"Maybe you're allergic to sex."

She returned his ironic smile.

"Fat chance."

After she left, he got to his feet, pulled on his clothes and shoes, grabbed his coat and walked down the hallway to the elevator. The lobby was empty except for the desk clerk. Stepping outside, he saw that Connie's Dodge was gone.

As he walked across the lot to his BMW, he noticed, farther down the row, a pick-up truck that was parked by itself. A camper shell rose above the cab. Someone was sitting behind the steering wheel. All Micah could see was an outline in the darkness.

When, two weeks later, they met again at the hotel's bar, Connie was anxious.

"My doctor didn't know what to make of that rash," she said. "So he sent me to a dermatologist. It has her stumped, too. Now another one has appeared on my arm." She pulled up the sleeve of her blouse to show him.

"Do you still want to get a room tonight?" he said.

"What's the matter—afraid I'm contagious?"

"I don't want to hurt you."

"I've got everything figured out," she said matter-of-factly. "If we do it doggy style, you won't be touching the front of my thigh or my lower arm.

"Besides, what's a little pain between lovers?"

TWENTY-FOUR.

The taxi from the airport dropped Micah and Comstock off in front of the State Capitol on a brilliant spring morning. They stood before a magnificent nineteenth century Neoclassical edifice that resembled nothing so much as the U.S. Capitol in Washington, D.C.

Adjacent to this building was a massive and characterless eight story structure. The offices of most legislators, including Senator Lee Grossman, were located in what Sacramento insiders called "the new building".

Once they entered, Micah led his companion through a maze of hallways and stairs. "They don't make it easy for their constituents to find them, do they?" Comstock observed as the pair rounded a corner.

Suddenly they stood at the doorway to Grossman's office. Even though he was one of the Senate's most powerful members, the reception area was surprisingly unassuming, with barely enough space for the secretary's desk and two State-issued chairs.

Before they had a chance to use them, Sute appeared from around a corner and motioned for the two to follow him.

The senator sat behind a large desk as they entered the old man's private office. His tiny frame practically disappeared into his plush leather chair. This room was quite different: expansive, with a row of huge windows facing the striking greenery of the Capitol's grounds.

Grossman didn't stand. As Micah and Comstock introduced themselves, they leaned across the desk in order to shake his hand. He stared blankly while they and Sute tried to settle into three uncomfortable wooden chairs.

"Lee, these are the individuals who have been working on the land saver project," Sute said.

"I know." He watched Micah through his thick eyeglasses.

"Have you read my legislation?"

"Yes. Numerous times."

"Let's see what you have."

With an effort, the senator raised himself from the chair and moved, with the others, to a maple table in a corner of the room.

Micah pulled the drawings out of the red leather case Ellen had loaned him and spread them on the table's surface. Grossman stood across from him while the assistant superintendent used the site plan to describe the relationship of the high school to the shopping center and showed the buildings' floor plans to the old man. Then Micah flipped to the last several sheets, which contained exterior renderings.

Ellen and her staff had given the two structures a strikingly contemporary appearance. Long, exposed steel girders, painted red, bisected walls. Balconies with cubist metal grillwork ran along the top floors. Stacks of long, narrow windows wrapped around corners.

The most conspicuous element, though, was the smaller building's east elevation. This stone facade faced Raymond Avenue, making it the most visible part of the school for those driving past on the street. Rising from its foundation, the wall slanted dramatically outward while climbing to the top of the roof, one hundred and twenty feet in the air. It looked like nothing so much as the bow of a gigantic ship.

When Micah finished going through every sheet, the senator raised his head.

"Go back to the site plan."

The old man carefully studied this for a moment.

"The school and the shopping center are next to each other on the same site. I'm looking for a project that literally shares the same piece of land with another use."

He glanced at Sute. "Like the school that was going to be built in the parking lot at Dodger Stadium. It would have been raised above ground level, so the baseball fans could park under it."

"Senator," Micah said, "what if we elevated this building"—he pointed at the smaller structure—"and had parking for the shopping center beneath the classrooms?"

Grossman looked him in the eyes.

"That would be better. Yeah, that's more like what I was thinking of."

For a moment, there was silence in the room.

"We're very interested in using your legislation to build this school," Micah said. "What should we do next?"

Sute spoke up. "Senator, what if the district sends a letter to the Disbursement Board, indicating that they're submitting a pilot project? They could include these plans plus a property appraisal, a site survey and an environmental assessment."

"That sounds all right." Grossman turned to Micah. "But I want to see the revised site plan, with the parking under the school, before you send the letter to the Board."

Once the visitors left Grossman's office, Comstock stopped in the middle of the empty hallway. There was an uneasy expression on his face.

"How are we going to keep the school and center separated if the Plaza patrons park under the classroom building?" he said impatiently.

"The only way to access those spaces will be from the Plaza. Even pedestrians won't be able to reach the parking garage from the campus."

Micah watched the developer.

"Now you have your thirty parking spaces. And we can tell Don Smith to stick it where the sun don't shine."

Comstock grinned and shook the other's hand.

"Good work, partner. And we didn't have to go to hell after all."

Micah leered at him.

"That's true. But Sacramento comes pretty fucking close."

The pair crossed the street and entered a large hotel. At the lobby's corner was the entrance to a steak house filled with lobbyists and their clients. The hostess led the men to a darkened booth.

When the martinis arrived, Micah and Comstock toasted to the successful meeting with the senator.

"We're home free now," Comstock said.

"Not yet. The School Board hasn't approved the project. And someone in the community could still file a lawsuit to try and stop it."

"I don't think that'll happen. Even Betty will know when she's beat."

Comstock set down his glass. "When Sute mentioned an environmental assessment, it reminded me of something I need to tell you."

"What's that?" Micah asked warily.

"There used to be a gas station where I put up the new building. When we demolished it, we also removed the underground fuel tanks. One of them had leaked in the past, and the spill migrated north. But the plume didn't reach the property I'm selling to you."

Micah stared at Comstock. He was remembering Fred Foster's diatribe.

"Are you sure the spill never got to the parking lot?"

"That's what my environmental consultant tells me."

"Then it shouldn't be a problem," Micah said. But this revelation worried him. Picking up his martini, he took a long swallow.

After the men finished another drink and shared two bottles of expensive Napa Cabernet during lunch, they took a taxi to the airport and found a bar near their departure gate. The pair slumped onto adjacent stools and ordered a round of cocktails.

"Can I ask you something?" Comstock said, slurring his words and smiling crookedly.

Even though he was having trouble holding his head up, Micah met his companion's bloodshot eyes.

"If you're able to pull this off—you know, get the land saver money and build the school—will that make you the greatest school planner in the state?"

Micah scowled at Comstock.

"What do you think?" he demanded belligerently.

Comstock grinned while the other customers looked over to see what the commotion was about. Unsteadily, he raised his glass as high as his arm would reach.

"To the greatest!"

As Comstock's hand swayed in the air, most of the gin splashed over the rim and sprayed the bar's surface.

"Bartender!" he shouted. "Can't you see my glass is empty?

"Another round!"

TWENTY-FIVE.

When Micah returned from Sacramento, he and the superintendent began to reach out to the community.

Dr. Hernandez served on the Chamber of Commerce's board of directors. "If we're going to have a well-educated workforce in the future, we have to build a high school," he told the other directors. Then Comstock, who was also a board member, asked the executives and business owners to adopt a resolution in support of the school. It passed without a dissenting vote. However, several of the members who lived north of the Plaza disappeared from the room before the roll was taken.

At his monthly meeting with the PTA leaders, the superintendent asked Micah to explain the land saver project. After he finished, Dr. Hernandez told the parents the district would be designating the future campus as a fundamental school.

"What does fundamental mean?" the superintendent asked rhetorically. "It means a high school where the focus will be on the basics of an exceptional educational experience. A school with a small student body, so the teaching staff can concentrate on individualized learning. A school that parents and their teenagers choose; this will create a positive energy and team spirit. And a school with a strict code of conduct, including a promise by parents to review and sign all homework assignments and limit the number of hours of television their teenagers watch every night.

"This school will be about excellence, commitment and involvement."

The parents looked at one another. They had never heard of such a school before—and an innovative academic initiative was not what they expected from Dr. Hernandez. Everyone knew the Board hired him to create a construction program.

"This is really exciting," said Denise Evans. "I'm sure our parents will love having an option like this."

Several of the others nodded in agreement.

Chimalma Acevedo, the only Latina at the table and the youngest person in the room, raised her hand.

"If there isn't enough space for everyone, how will the district choose who goes there?" she asked Dr. Hernandez.

"At other schools of choice around the state, students register on a first-come, first-serve basis, or else their names are drawn in a lottery."

Denise spoke again. "Tell us more about the code of conduct."

"The students must stay out of the Plaza and park only on district property."

"Will there be a lot for them at the school?" another mother asked.

"There isn't enough acreage in the shopping center," the superintendent said. "But the district will provide parking nearby."

In fact, he had scheduled a meeting with Micah, Denise and Amber Young, the principal of Raymond Avenue Elementary, for later that morning to discuss this very topic.

Micah began the second meeting by unrolling a plan of the Raymond Avenue campus. The existing parking lot and structures, including the multi-purpose building which was under construction, were clustered at the site's north end. In place of the portable classrooms, the plan showed a new building.

Tucked by itself into the property's southeast corner was the lot for the high school students.

"Dr. Hernandez went over this plan with me last week," Amber told Denise. "I think our school will function better because of it. We won't have classrooms spread all over the site. That'll improve communication and security."

The principal, a small woman in her mid-thirties with long blonde hair, turned to Micah. "Speaking of security, I'm concerned about teenagers sharing the site."

"A fence will surround the new parking lot, and keep it separated from the playfield," he said.

Denise spoke for the first time since the meeting began.

"I've talked with Micah about getting rid of the portable classrooms. His plan takes care of that issue while giving the high school students some place to park. I like what he's shown us."

At the meeting's end, Micah and Denise left the superintendent's office together and walked outside.

"Thanks for your support," he said.

"I'm happy to do my part."

He couldn't keep his eyes off her. She was the most attractive woman he had ever met.

"I want to tell you more about the new classroom building. Can we go to lunch some time?"

A Mona Lisa smile crossed her face.

"I'd like that."

When Micah returned to the facility department, Keona stood to meet him.

"There's someone waiting for you," she said. "She's been here quite a while."

Moving to his office, he saw that Chimalma was sitting in front of his desk. Besides being a parent leader, the short, plump woman was also, like Micah, an employee of the district.

After Dr. Hernandez arrived, it didn't take long for him to realize that few of the Latino parents were involved in the district's activities. There was the lack of participation in the PTA. But they were also mostly absent at parent-teacher conference days and school open houses; it was difficult, too, for principals to find enough parent volunteers to assist with the supervision of students during field trips.

"How can we meet the needs of our parents if they have such a tenuous connection to the district?" he asked the cabinet members.

The superintendent was concerned, too, that this lack of engagement would carry over to the local bond campaign. State law required two-thirds of the community's voters to approve the property tax increase. For the measure to be successful, the campaign needed as many parents as possible to speak out and, if they were citizens, go to the polls.

After much thought and multiple conversations with principals and community members, Dr. Hernandez developed a plan for building bridges between the Latino parents and their children's schools. The district would provide transportation to its school activities. It would begin compensating parents who took part in field trips. And it would hire a group of parents to coordinate these services and develop additional initiatives.

Chimalma was one of the first candidates who Dr. Hernandez interviewed to be a parent coordinator. She kept her eyes on him as they shook hands and sat across from one another.

"Tell me about yourself," he said.

"I was born in Mexico, and moved to the States when I was a teenager. I'm a single mother; my son is eight years old."

"Where did you come from?"

"A very small village along the coast. My father's a fisherman."

"Why did you leave Mexico?"

She hesitated. "I thought my son would have a brighter future north of the border."

"Do you still believe that's the case?"

"Yes. He has good teachers and loves to learn. I'm at his school almost every day, volunteering to do what I can to help out."

She shifted in the chair. "But many of the other parents don't see the importance of being part of their children's education. They need someone they trust to lead the way. That's why I want to be a coordinator."

"Is there anything else I should know about you?" he said. "Perhaps a talent that the other applicants don't possess."

"I can see what others can't," she said proudly.

He leaned forward. "What do you mean?"

"Even on the blackest night, I can see in the dark. It's a gift that God gave me when I was a little girl."

Dr. Hernandez smiled at her in spite of himself. "Well, we could use a little magic around here," he said.

One morning during his first month at the district, Micah was called to the superintendent's office. Sitting around the conference table with Dr. Hernandez were the five newly hired parent coordinators, including Chimalma.

"These ladies are going to show our mothers and fathers the district belongs to them," the superintendent said. "I want you to help them in any way you can."

They tried to spread the word about the importance of the bond measure. But the Latino parents' lack of English fluency and legal status stood in the way of their ability or willingness to engage with the campaign. In the end, the property tax increase won overwhelming approval. However, the community's Latinos played a minor role in this outcome.

Micah and the coordinators met on the afternoon after the election.

"The next time something comes along that's good for our families," Chimalma told the others, "we need to make our voices heard."

He remembered these words as he stepped behind his cluttered desk and sat across from her.

"Why is the new school going to be so small?" She spoke with a thick accent.

"Fairview Plaza doesn't have enough land for anything more."

"If this is going to be the best school in the district, do you think the Anglo parents will send their kids there, instead of to the private schools?"

"No one can answer that question," he said. "Not yet, anyway."

"It would be a sin if the white kids took all the seats. But first things first."

She paused, staring at him.

"I need your help. Our parents must know about the new school. I'm going to set up meetings all over the city. Can you come and tell them about it?"

Micah returned Chimalma's gaze.

"I'll be at every meeting," he promised.

TWENTY-SIX.

Soon after the trip to the State Capitol, Micah compiled the information Sute told him to submit to the Disbursement Board. He flew to Sacramento again to show Senator Grossman the revised conceptual drawings, with the thirty parking spaces located under the smaller classroom building.

When he arrived at Grossman's office, an aide was waiting for him.

"The Senate's in session today," the young man said. "We'll be meeting the senator at the Capitol."

Micah followed him through a confusing series of narrow passageways that connected the two buildings. After a few minutes, they came to a doorway manned by a plainclothes security officer. He looked into the red leather case before motioning them to proceed.

Suddenly, they were on the floor of the Senate chamber. Decorated in nineteenth century opulence, the grand, high-ceilinged space included rows of Greek columns, ruby carpeting and two huge chandeliers that hung over the center of the circular room.

One of the Senate's officers stood on a stage-like rostrum, reading aloud the contents of a pending bill. None of the senators seemed to be listening; they were clustered in small groups, arguing among themselves, and sitting at their oak desks, studying sheaves of documents.

Above their heads, several dozen visitors looked down from the second floor gallery, trying to make sense of democracy at work.

As Micah and the aide stood near the entrance door, Grossman suddenly appeared out of the chamber's chaos. The old man was even shorter than Micah remembered. Without a word, the senator took him by the elbow and led him to a wooden shelf which was mounted against a nearby wall.

While Grossman watched, Micah took a single sheet from the case. He spread it on the shelf and pointed out where the shopping center's customers would park under the school building.

Studying the sheet, the old man nudged his glasses up his bulbous nose. After a moment, he turned to Micah.

"This looks okay," he muttered.

Then he turned and disappeared again among his fellow senators.

Micah walked several blocks to an impressive granite-faced building where the State Disbursement Board's staff occupied the entire fourth floor. When he stepped out of the elevator, Sute was waiting. The big man led him to a small conference room. Micah handed Sute a large brown envelope, stuffed with papers. Sute read the cover letter and flipped through the various documents before he raised his head.

"I'll get the staff working on this right away," he said.

TWENTY-SEVEN.

It was dusk when Micah parked his BMW sedan behind Chimalma's dented Ford Fiesta in front of a two story apartment building. There were rental complexes up and down the road—a dozen multi-story buildings within his eyesight in the fading light.

When, during the late 1960's, the county decided to construct a massive new downtown courthouse, the city manager at the time convinced the Council that its presence would result in an influx of new residents. At his urging, the zoning designation near the courthouse site was amended to encourage the demolition of existing houses and the construction of apartment buildings in their place.

"Attorneys and executive secretaries and officers of the courts will move in," the city manager promised. "They will change the face of downtown. It will become the most vibrant part of the city, with new restaurants and shops to cater to the apartment dwellers."

Part of his prediction came true. A wave of new residents certainly arrived. But they didn't even know the courthouse existed. The apartments were filled with families who had trekked north from Mexico's impoverished farming villages in search of a better life. When the Council (including Myron Richland's father, who was mayor at the time) saw what had happened, it reversed the zone change and fired the city manager. He was replaced by Don Smith.

Micah climbed the exterior stairs and moved along a narrow landing to the apartment where he was to meet Chimalma and a group of parents, the fifth such gathering he had attended in the past two weeks.

When he knocked, he could hear scurrying behind the door before it finally swung open.

Chimalma stood in front of him.

"Come in," she said flatly, staring at him with her usual poker face.

The small living room was jammed with parents, many of whom still wore mechanic's overalls, maid uniforms and other work clothes. Some held small children in their arms. They sat against the room's bare walls in chairs of all shapes and sizes and on a huge, tattered sofa, studying the new arrival.

Chimalma introduced Micah in Spanish.

"It hasn't been easy to find someplace to build a high school for your children," he began. "But our search may be at an end."

After every few sentences, he stopped so Chimalma could interpret what he had said. He described the land saver funding, and how it would allow a school to be constructed at Fairview Plaza.

"Before we can build the school, though, the School Board must approve it."

"Is it true," asked a middle-aged man in Spanish, "that some people are trying to stop it?"

Micah nodded. He described the neighbors' concerns, and how the code of conduct and the new parking lot at Raymond Avenue Elementary were intended to placate them.

A young man spoke up in English. "I've heard our kids will have to win a lottery to get into the school."

"The Board hasn't made that decision yet. But a lottery is one way to make sure every student in the district has the same opportunity for a seat."

"How do we know Latinos have a fair chance of getting picked—that this isn't a rigged system set up to favor the white kids?"

"Dr. Hernandez will make sure it's fair," Micah said.

When they heard this, the parents nodded approvingly at one another.

Chimalma spoke again. In Spanish, she insisted that they go to the Board meetings and voice their support for the new high school.

"We'll only have ourselves to blame if this school doesn't get built," she said.

Spontaneously, the parents rose and surrounded Micah. He towered over everyone in the room. They smiled at him, and he shook their outstretched hands.

The young man followed Micah out the apartment's front door and onto the landing. Night had fallen; it was almost impossible to see.

"What's the odds you'll get the State money?" the Latino said.

"Better than fifty-fifty."

"I hope the bigots win and the school never gets built."

Micah couldn't believe what he was hearing.

"Why would you say that?" he stuttered impatiently. "Do you know what that would mean? The overcrowding could go on for decades."

The young man didn't back down. "It'd show everyone, once and for all, exactly how racist the system is in this city."

Micah began to calm down.

"What's your name?"

"Danny Aguilar."

"Danny, it's within the School Board's power to end the overcrowding. Working within the system—and convincing the Board to do the right thing—is the only way to get what you need. If you shun the system, you're only hurting yourselves."

"For centuries, the system you brag on has treated us like subhumans," he replied, his voice dripping with bitterness. "It's stolen our land and destroyed our gods.

"You and that stooge of a superintendent promise the lottery won't be rigged. But you're both a cog in an evil machine. Why should any of us believe one goddamn word you say?"

There was silence while the pair faced one another in the dark. Finally Micah turned from him and went down the stairs.

Crossing the street and approaching the BMW, he saw someone standing on the sidewalk next to the car. Even though it was a pleasant spring evening, the figure wore an ankle-length trench coat and a knit ski cap. Very tall and slim—reed-like, he thought—the apparition was holding a sheaf of papers in one hand.

Slipping behind the steering wheel, he began to adjust his rear view mirror. That was when he realized a pick-up truck with a camper shell was parked behind him.

A block after he'd pulled away from the curb, Micah noticed a flyer on the passenger-side windshield, tucked under the wiper blade and flapping against the glass. He braked the car, reached across the hood and grasped the paper. Back inside the BMW, he turned on the roof light and spread it across the steering wheel.

At the top of the flyer was a headline in large print letters. Micah set his jaw as he read:

CONNIE CARR IS UNFAITHFUL
TO HER HUSBAND—
AND TO YOU

According to the document, Connie was having affairs with numerous school district administrators. "And she rubber-stamps everything they present at the Board meetings—including their employment contracts and a harebrained scam for building a new high school.

"Is this who we want as our representative—a woman who throws away our tax dollars at the whim of her lovers?" it asked. "She's unfaithful to her husband, she's unfaithful to us—and she has GOT TO GO!"

Micah made a quick U-turn. When he reached the stretch of road where he saw the tall figure and the pick-up truck, they had both disappeared. He pulled to the curb.

Were Betty Phelan and the high school's opponents behind the flyer? And was the pick-up the same one he'd seen parked at the hotel? He sat there on the darkened street, pondering these questions—and wondering how he could find the answers—before he drove away.

TWENTY-EIGHT.

Since Phelan's appearance before the Board and the start of the district's outreach effort, the high school had become the number one topic of debate throughout the city.

Kent Hamish wrote several front page articles about the divisions it had created in the community. He interviewed everyone from Senator Grossman to Myron Richland, Betty Phelan and Sam Comstock.

Both opponents and supporters began to attend the board meetings. They stood in line behind the podium, waiting for their turn to speak. Sometimes, the queue stretched to the rear of the room. This portion of the meetings was now lasting two hours or more.

Those denouncing the school included residents from north of the shopping center and a handful of Fairview Plaza tenants, concerned that the campus' presence would chase away their customers. Sometimes, the opponents brought along their attorneys, who told the Board their clients were considering the legal options to stop what they described as "an ill-conceived scheme".

The naysayers were vastly outnumbered by supporters, most of whom were parents. Many didn't speak English. Chimalma or one of the other parent coordinators would stand beside them at the podium and interpret their pleas to build the school.

One evening, an old man rose from his chair at the back of the crowded room and got into the line of speakers. He was short and very thin, with white hair and a neatly trimmed gray moustache. After a half hour, his turn came to step to the podium.

"My name is Luciano Reynoso. I came here from Mexico fifty years ago to live with my sister." He spoke slowly and carefully.

"World War II was going on, and I joined the Army. Since I wanted to enjoy the benefits of living in this wonderful country, I felt I should also fight to defend it. I learned to speak English during basic training and with my outfit in North Africa and France.

"At the end of the war, I was discharged and came back here, where I met my wife. I also signed up with the Army Reserve. Five years later, when the fighting broke out in Korea, I was called to active duty. I served under General MacArthur in X Corps during the landing at Inchon.

"After I was discharged for the second time, my wife and I became U.S. citizens and raised our family in this city. My three daughters still live here. Now they have children of their own who are going to high school. I visit the campus every week to see my grandchildren play sports and perform at concerts."

The subdued tone of his voice suddenly changed.

"The conditions at that school are very poor," he said angrily. "My grandchildren have to wait in line so long to buy their lunch that they barely have time to eat it. Sometimes, it takes fifteen or twenty minutes for them to get into a restroom. They have to push their way through the other kids to get to their next class. Getting in to see a counselor takes months."

He stopped again and glowered at the Board members. "The overcrowding is out of control. You have got to build the new high school.

"I did my duty in Africa and Europe and Korea.

"Now it's your turn to do your duty."

The cramped room exploded in applause and raucous shouts of support while the Board members stared, stone faced, at the old man.

The Anglo parents also mentioned the overcrowding crisis, as well as the land saver funding. "I can't imagine anyone winning a jackpot who said 'Nah, I don't want the money.' That's stupid!" noted one white father excitedly.

But the Anglos spent just as much of their time speaking about the fundamental nature of the new school and the high standards it would foster.

"I have two sons. I sent the older one to a Catholic high school that cost more than I could afford. I didn't feel I had any choice if he was going to have a good education," said an Anglo mother. "If this school's built, I'll send his younger brother there."

As the speakers stepped to the podium and presented their entreaties, the Board members sat silently. Every time a question was asked, Richland recited the same answer: "State law prohibits us from responding because the project isn't listed on the meeting's agenda."

In closed session, Yeoman and Laird pressured Richland to place the land saver school on an upcoming agenda.

"This is the most important issue we've ever dealt with," Yeoman said. "The public should know what each of us thinks about it."

The Board president shook his head.

"We aren't even sure if we're going to receive the land saver funding. Once it's clear the project can actually be built, we'll definitely review it in open session."

In reality, any Board member could request that a subject be placed on a meeting agenda. For some reason, Yeoman had chosen not to take this step. Micah thought she didn't want to be perceived as the leader of the opposition. The project's christening as a fundamental school put her in a complicated situation.

During her election campaign, she demanded that the district create schools of choice with strict codes of conduct. Finally, the majority of the Board was supporting this vision—but at a school that Yeoman's supporters, many of whom lived north of the Plaza, were adamantly opposed to ever seeing constructed.

Behind closed doors, Yeoman and Laird also insisted that Micah be directed to find alternative sites. "In a city this large, there have to be other properties that wouldn't get everyone so upset," claimed Laird.

In order to placate the pair, Micah was directed to prepare a confidential review of all possible sites. After a lengthy debate, the Board determined—at Dr. Hernandez's urging—that the report would only include locations which meet the land saver law's criteria.

Only four Board members gave Micah this direction. Connie no longer attended the meetings. The last time they had met at the hotel, there were sores, rashes and lesions all over her body. They tried to make love, but every position they attempted caused her too much pain to go on.

"I can't find a doctor who knows what's wrong with me," she told him as they lay in bed. "Last week, I visited a specialist at Scripps Institute. He was as baffled as all the others."

Despite the discomfort it caused her, she pressed against him.

"I'm scared, Micah," she whispered.

Then she began to sob.

TWENTY-NINE.

Micah was sitting at his desk, working on the report to the Board, when his phone rang.

"Mr. Wada, Fred Foster here."

This was a call Micah had been dreading.

"We're both busy men, so let me get to the point. I received your submittal for the high school at the shopping center, and I have two serious concerns with it.

"First, the environmental assessment indicates a leaking underground fuel tank is on the site."

"The tank was removed over three years ago," Micah said. "And it wasn't located on the land we're purchasing."

He could hear a shuffling as Foster flipped through the document.

"But there's a fuel plume which has been migrating towards the school site for years."

"It never reached the site and has stopped moving."

"Who's to say the plume couldn't start moving again?" Foster said impatiently.

Micah pressed the fingers of his right hand against his temple.

"Our environmental consultant thinks that's highly unlikely. Still, the property owner has agreed to install a series of monitoring wells at the edge of the site."

"The most important part of my job is making sure students and their teachers aren't exposed to health hazards because of a district's actions," Foster said. "If the soil is contaminated, those at the school could inhale the vapors. As I'm sure you know, that would lead to a heightened risk of cancer.

"I'm going to insist that you retain another environmental consultant to review the assessment."

Frowning at his notepad, Micah didn't respond. He knew what Foster was hoping to do: kill the project with a thousand cuts. When, months later, the second environmental assessment confirmed the property was safe, the State bureaucrat would be ready with new demands.

"My second concern is with the cost of the land," Foster said. "All three appraisals greatly inflate its value."

"The appraisers were selected because they've been estimating property values for decades."

"I have twenty years of experience in the real world," Foster snapped. "Twenty years as a commercial real estate agent and developer." He sounded as though he was on the verge of losing control of himself.

"You're telling me the State should pay eighteen million dollars for a parking lot. That's outrageous."

"But the property wasn't appraised as a parking lot. Its highest and best use is as part of a shopping center. Someday, a big box store could be constructed on that land if we don't purchase it."

"Eighteen million dollars is outrageous," Foster repeated.

The line was silent for a moment.

"I'll be sending you a letter by the end of the month with my concerns," Foster said. Then he hung up.

Micah dialed Sute's number.

"Shit!" the big man growled after Micah told him what had happened. "Let me go talk to him."

Later that afternoon, Sute called Micah back.

"As I told you in San Diego, the guy's out of control. He won't listen to reason. In the end, the Disbursement Board will approve your project—I can guarantee that. This is Lee's baby, and he has the votes."

"But Foster's bullshit will scare the living daylights out of the School Board members," Micah said.

"With any luck, they'll never know about it."

Micah didn't see how that could happen. At the very least, he would have to tell the Board about Foster's letter when it arrived. And he was certain of how Betty Phelan would use the State official's implications when Violet Yeoman passed the correspondence along. Kent Hamish would receive a phone call as soon as the councilwoman had the letter in her hands.

THIRTY.

When Micah called Denise to arrange their lunch, she suggested they meet at a country club in a nearby city. "When my husband and I divorced, I got the club membership," she explained.

Micah drove north on the congested freeway for twenty minutes before he steered the BMW down an offramp and onto a wide boulevard. It was lined with towering office buildings and upscale shopping malls.

After a few miles, he turned up a two lane road that scaled a steep hill. Climbing the grade, the car passed sprawling houses on either side. At the top of the rise stood a tall masonry wall and a guard shack. Frowning, the security guard squinted at him. When Micah said he was meeting Denise Evans for lunch, the man grabbed a clipboard and reviewed it for a moment before grudgingly waving him through.

Suddenly he was on the edge of a compact valley whose ridgelines were surmounted by mansions of various configurations and architectural styles. Below them, a golf course stretched over most of the valley's floor. The bright midday sunlight that flooded this scene, reflecting off the mansions' windows and the course's water hazards, made it seem otherworldly.

In the distance was the clubhouse and restaurant. Micah spotted Denise's white Audi station wagon, parked near the building's entrance. She was studying her scorecard at a table with a view of the eighteenth hole as he walked into the room. When she saw him, she stood and, smiling warmly, extended her hand.

She wore a white skort and tight, sleeveless turquoise shirt. Her long, slim legs accentuated her curvaceous figure.

He glanced out the window as they sat down.

"This is a beautiful view."

And this is a gorgeous woman, he told himself as he turned back to her.

"It's my favorite table."

"Did you play this morning?"

She nodded, a frown on her face.

"Although not very well. Do you play?"

Coming from her lips, that question
Sent his imagination racing,
Set off a fantasy
That wasn't about golf—
A fantasy
Involving she and him
And a long afternoon
Nude and lying together
Limbs entwined
On a narrow bed
In a very private room.

"I've tried it a few times," he said. "It takes a lot of time and effort to be good, doesn't it?"

"In my case, it takes a lot of time and effort to be subpar."

"I can't imagine you being subpar at anything."

She smiled and said: "I'm glad you asked me to lunch. Since the bond campaign, we haven't had a chance to talk."

"How's your family?" he asked.

"Oh, they're fine. They love Raymond Avenue. Amber is such a great principal."

"How old are your kids now?"

"Joseph is almost twelve; Janelle is nine; and Janice is six."

"So Joseph is going into seventh grade in September?"

She nodded. "That'll be a big change."

"Which intermediate school is he going to attend?"

"The parents in our neighborhood chose a private school in Irvine. Keeping the boys and girls together who have known each other all their lives is important to us."

"I've heard that none of the kids from your part of town go on to Madison Intermediate," Micah said.

"The parents think Madison's neighborhood isn't safe."

"On the weekends, families from all over the county attend classical music concerts in Madison's auditorium," he said. "They must feel safe, or they wouldn't go there."

She set her azure eyes on him. "Sometimes, assumptions can be as important as reality. My ex-husband is involved in politics. He says assumptions are the trump card on election day."

"What do you mean when you say 'involved'?"

"He was the single biggest donor to the governor's last campaign."

Micah raised his eyebrows. "That must have been a very big check."

They hadn't taken their eyes from one another since he arrived.

"Mind if I ask you a personal question?" he said.

"No. I don't mind."

"Are you dating anyone?"

"I'm dating several guys. Why do you ask?"

"Would you like to go to dinner sometime?"

"Sure. I'd love to." She paused. "I just wonder why it took you so long to ask me out."

He shrugged. "You know me. I'm the shy, retiring type."

She narrowed her eyes. "For some reason, I don't remember ever seeing that side of you."

THIRTY-ONE.

As soon as Micah opened the mailbox in front of his house, he spotted a plain white business size envelope in the pile of advertising flyers and marketing letters. Postmarked in Hammonton, it was addressed with the familiar large block letters.

The unsigned note inside was printed on a small slip of tan paper. All it said was YOU WILL BE READING ABOUT ME.

Micah walked quickly up the lawn, unlocked the front door and strode to the phone.

"I was just about to call you," Petersen said. "A reporter from the Oregonian visited here last week. She spent quite a bit of time interviewing folks about the crime wave.

"I hope you're sitting down. She talked to the thief."

Micah felt a shiver go through his body.

Anxiously, he asked: "Did she tell you anything about that?"

"Not much. Reporters don't share information with law enforcement. That violates their code of ethics." It sounded like Petersen didn't think much of these ethics.

"Did she say when the story would be published?"

"This week."

"Can you give me her name and phone number?"

Petersen reached for a business card at the edge of the desk.

"Her name's Stacey Sanders." After he recited the reporter's number into the mouthpiece, the chief stood, still holding the phone to his ear, and looked through his office's open doorway.

"I think I see today's paper setting on the front counter. Hold on a minute."

He brought it back to his desk and spread it before him. Then Petersen picked up the phone.

"It's in today's edition."

"I'd like to see it as soon as I can."

"How about if I fax it to you?"

"Let me give you the number for the machine at my office."

Once Petersen confirmed the story had been sent, Micah rushed out to the BMW, pulled onto the freeway and raced back to the school district headquarters through the river of cars.

He walked briskly across the empty bullpen to the fax machine. The pages were waiting for him. Micah scooped them up, went into his office and sat down behind his cluttered desk.

The headline said: Young Man Sails Into Trouble.

His hands trembled as he began to read.

"For the last two years, a teenager has single-handedly perpetrated a crime wave in the two-state region that borders the mouth of the Columbia River," the article began. "He has burglarized everything from markets and hardware stores to a fire station (to steal night vision goggles, say authorities) and broken into numerous vacation houses.

"The young bandit has even gained a nickname—the 'sailing thief'—for his habit of stealing various types of watercraft to make his getaways.

"'Frankly, we've never seen anything like it before,' admitted Hugh Dervish, the sheriff of Washington state's Pacific County. 'When someone's escape route is the entire river, it's tough to track him down.'

"The sailing thief's identity has been a mystery since the crimes began. Law enforcement officers have caught nothing more than brief glimpses of him in the flesh. The only photos that exist are grainy images from surveillance cameras at the businesses he has robbed. They show a tall, thin, ghost-like figure, his arms filled with dry goods, groceries and bottles of Coke—apparently his drink of choice.

"However, the Oregonian was able to interview the bandit last week. At a secluded location in the woods of northwest Oregon, he described an odyssey which has consumed the last four years of his young life.

"'I ran away from my home in Southern California when I was fourteen,' said the lanky teenager, who calls himself a single name, Welund. 'I'm eighteen now, so I've been on my own for a long time.'

"Welund says that he became a runaway because 'things were messed up at home.' His father, an official at a school district, spent so much time at work that, growing up, the boy rarely saw him. The relationship between father and son began to deteriorate when Welund's mother contracted breast cancer and died after a long and painful struggle. 'After my mom passed away, there was no one who cared about me. That's when I decided to get out,' he explained.

"First, he lived in a homeless encampment under a bridge along the Los Angeles River. Welund stumbled upon the camp while hitchhiking around the region, trying to figure out how he would live on his own. 'It was a scary place,' he noted.

"Among those who he met was a young man with long black hair who proclaimed himself a 'prophet of God' and gave Welund a paperback Bible. 'We all have a God-shaped hole in us,' the man told him. 'That hole can only be filled by faith. Read the Good Book and pray to the Lord and he will show you a purpose for your life.'

"One night, Welund was awakened by gunshots down the river. Someone had murdered three men and two women at another encampment. 'Everyone said it was a drug deal gone bad,' the teenager remembered. 'After that happened, I packed up my stuff and left.'

"Welund hitchhiked to Las Vegas because 'I'd never been there before and had always heard about it.' Hanging out with other homeless teens, he found out about a network of flood control tunnels that ran for miles under the city. 'Dozens of people live down there,' he said. Welund soon joined them. Every morning, he would awaken in the tunnels and step through a series of passageways and corridors until he was outside, standing in the blinding sunlight.

"'I begged in front of the casinos and slipped inside of them when I could, looking for slot machines with credits to play or winnings that had been left behind.' Once, he pulled the lever of a slot machine with a leftover credit and hit a $125 jackpot.

"The time in Las Vegas ended when, early one morning, he heard the sound of running water rushing through the tunnels. Overnight, a summer monsoon unleashed a deluge on the city. As Welund lay in his sleeping bag in the dark, a wall of water churned over him. 'I was swept along and couldn't get out of the sleeping bag,' the teenager remembered. 'I thought I was going to drown.' Fortunately, he was pushed into a pile of debris; this gave him the chance to struggle, coughing and choking, out of the bag as the waist-deep torrent continued to rush by. But he lost his Bible in the deluge.

"'I could have kept living in Vegas,' he said. 'There were lots of other homeless kids there; they slept in abandoned buildings and parks. But I didn't want to live out on the streets. It seemed too dangerous.'

"So Welund hit the road again—this time, back to Southern California. The runaway had been so successful as a panhandler in the desert that he paid for a ride on a Greyhound bus. When he arrived at the Los Angeles depot, he was approached by a member of the Travelers Aid Society, who directed him to the Teen Canteen, a lounge staffed with volunteer counselors. One of them told Welund about a halfway house for runaways in Hollywood.

"He moved in that afternoon and soon learned about a community garden a few blocks away that was seeking volunteers to help elderly residents from the surrounding apartment buildings tend their crops. 'Here I was in the middle of this big, grungy city without a friend in the world,' Welund remembered, 'but working in the garden gave me a feeling of tranquility. It sounds weird, but I felt like I'd found a home.'

"The teenager became close to several of the seniors who he was assisting at the garden, including a former actor who urged the runaway to decide what he wanted to do with his life. 'The old man used to say: "You'll never again have so much freedom. Take advantage of it".' At the same time, his roommate at the halfway house, a native of northwest Oregon, told him the region was 'like the end of the world—a place where no one will bother you, where you don't have to feel afraid.'

"The pair decided to leave the halfway house and Southern California and headed north. They rode freight trains for much of the journey. Just past the California-Oregon border, however, they became separated when Welund jumped into an open boxcar but his companion couldn't keep up with the train as it picked up speed.

"Alone, Welund reached Astoria on a cold, blustery after-noon; it was the first time he saw the Columbia River. He traveled into the underpopulated area to the west between the city and the ocean—where his crime spree began. For two years, he has evaded law enforcement authorities in two states.

"'I'm not a bad person,' the teenager says when asked about the numerous burglaries and thefts that he admits committing. 'I haven't hurt anyone—I don't even have a gun. I'm on my own, and I don't have any place to go. So I'm making my way in this world the best that I can. I guess you could say that I'm still looking for a purpose in my life.'"

Micah stared at the page. Then he set the article on top of the mismatched clumps of memos, letters and reports that covered his desk.

I've let my boy down for a long time, he thought, staring into the artificial light that flooded the bullpen.

I'm not going to let him down any longer.

THIRTY-TWO.

The next morning, Micah closed the door to his office and dialed Stacey Sanders' number.

"I'm calling about the story you worked on last week in Hammonton."

"What do you have to tell me?" she asked, slowly and softly.

"I think the young man you wrote about is my son."

"And what makes you say that?"

Micah recounted his disappearance four years before and the recent arrival of the two handwritten notes.

"Is he all right?"

"The last two years have been very hard. You can imagine— on the run while the region's law enforcement agencies conducted an intensive manhunt."

"I think about it every day," he said. "Tell me how to contact him."

"I can't. It would compromise my integrity as a reporter. I promise everyone I interview that I'll never share anything they tell me unless it was on the record."

"Look, Stacey, we both know his life's at risk," Micah replied impatiently. "Either by drowning in the Columbia River. Or from the revolver of a nervous deputy sheriff. I'm the one person who can convince him to surrender to the authorities before something tragic happens."

For a moment, he heard nothing on the line. Then the reporter spoke up.

"Just southwest of Astoria is a state park with a replica of Fort Clatsop. That's where I met your son—if that's who Welund is. It was just blind luck I found him. Another runaway I talked to in Astoria told me the fort is where the homeless teenagers cross paths."

She wasn't telling Micah the truth. In fact, Welund initiated their communication by calling her and offering to meet. The fugitive even gave the reporter a phone number where he could be reached. In the process of arranging their meeting, she dialed the number twice. The first time, Welund answered the phone. The second time, a teenage girl's voice came on the line. When Sanders asked for Welund, she offered to take a message. The next day, he called the reporter back and told her to come to the fort.

"What was Fort Clatsop?" Micah said.

"After the members of the Lewis and Clark expedition reached the Pacific Ocean, they constructed it as shelter for the winter. During the three months they spent there, it rained constantly. The men suffered from colds and flu, their clothes rotted and fleas infested the blankets and hides they used as bedding."

When the call ended, Micah stood and reopened the office's door. Standing before him was Kent Hamish.

"Got a couple of minutes?" the reporter asked. "I have something to show you."

As soon as they were seated in his office, Hamish thrust a multi-page letter at him across the desk's chaos. The pages were upside down, and Micah fumbled with them for a few seconds before realizing the first page was on the State Disbursement Board's letterhead.

It was addressed to him.

He flipped to the last page and saw Fred Foster's signature. Below this was a list of cc's, including Betty Phelan, Don Smith—and Hamish.

According to Foster's letter, the fuel plume would put the health and safety of teachers and their students at risk and the appraisals established a value for the parking lot that bore no relationship to sound business practices and common sense.

He felt a flash of panic—and then a rush of anger.

"Is there any truth to Foster's claims?" Hamish opened his notepad as he spoke.

"Can we talk off the record?"

The reporter stared at him. "Okay," he said, closing the notepad.

"This guy has an ax to grind. He's feuding with other people in Sacramento. And our district has gotten caught in the middle."

Micah explained the dispute between the governor and Lee Grossman over the future bond measure. "Foster was sent to the Disbursement Board to punish the senator," he said.

"That may be true." Hamish opened his notepad again. "But you haven't answered my question."

Stacked on the floor next to the desk were the environmental assessment and the three property appraisals. The assistant superintendent bent down and, with some effort, hoisted the voluminous documents into his arms.

"Follow me," he told Hamish.

The pair walked to the conference room and sat at the tables. Micah showed Hamish the environmental assessment's conclusion. Then he opened each appraisal, turned to the executive summaries and shoved them in front of the reporter.

"I have to deal with facts," Micah said while Hamish scribbled on the notepad. "The facts prove the site is clean and safe and the value of the property is eighteen million dollars."

"I'm going to talk to your consultants and the others who received the letter," Hamish said.

"I hope you do. By the way, do you mind if I make a copy? After all, it's addressed to me."

As soon as the reporter departed, Micah dialed Dr. Hernandez's line. He described what Foster had done—composed a letter full of fabrications and sent it to Hamish and the project's opponents.

"I have a copy for you," Micah said.

"Bring it over."

The superintendent sat at the conference table. Across from him was Glenn Woodson, another assistant superintendent. A small, balding man who wore wire-rimmed glasses, he had worked at the district for many years. Woodson was responsible for management of the two high schools and the district's intermediate schools.

Over the last few weeks, Micah and Ellen had been working intently with Woodson and a group of administrators and teachers to define the fundamental campus' education program. Woodson had never before been involved in planning a new school—much less the community's first fundamental school. During the committee's meetings, he made no attempt to hide his resentment at having to participate in the endeavor. He always showed up late and left before they finished. And he raised objections to most of Micah's suggestions—but never offered advice and direction of his own.

Woodson ignored Micah as he entered the room. The little man was in the midst of explaining to Dr. Hernandez why the upcoming high school graduation ceremonies needed to begin in the afternoon, rather than the traditional time in the evening. Micah stood in a corner of the office as Woodson told the superintendent how the later start would delay the beginning of summer vacation for the schools' staffs.

As he listened to this monologue, Dr. Hernandez began to tap his index finger impatiently on the table top. Finally, he interrupted Woodson.

"Isn't the later time more convenient for the parents? It gives them a chance to get home from work and greet the relatives who have come from out of town for the occasion."

"But Jim—"

The superintendent raised his hand. "Micah called and asked to speak with me before you came in. Can we finish this up later?"

Woodson frowned. "All right. But we need to make a decision soon. The graduations will be upon us before we know it."

As he left the office, he walked past Micah as if the latter didn't exist.

"Glenn's not happy with you," Dr. Hernandez said while Micah took the seat that Woodson had vacated. "He tells me you've hijacked the planning committee."

Micah grimaced and looked up at the office's ceiling, as if begging somebody up there to rescue him from the district's bureaucrats. Then he turned his eyes to his boss.

"Once the Disbursement Board approves our project, we'll be expected to quickly submit a more detailed set of plans to the State. All I'm trying to do is keep the process moving forward. I don't know if Glenn understands what's at stake."

"Well, he's a ball of fire when it comes to deciding if summer vacation should start a few hours early."

Micah handed Foster's letter to the superintendent. When he finished reading it, Dr. Hernandez set the pages down on the table and shook his head.

"Things were starting to go our way," he said lowly. "Most of the folks I've talked to support the idea of a fundamental high school. Now..."

His voice trailed off.

"But the site isn't contaminated, and we're not going to pay too much for it," Micah said.

"You and I know that. But will the public understand? Will they believe us?"

He held up the first page of the letter. "This came from the State of California, and was signed by a State official."

Micah watched the superintendent.

"Jim, there's something else I have to talk with you about. Something that's very important."

"What is it?" The old man sounded weary.

"My son is in serious trouble."

Micah told the story of Benjamin's disappearance and the unexpected letter from Oregon. He described the phone calls to Chief Petersen and the conversation with Stacey Sanders.

"I think he's in mortal danger," Micah said. "I've got to fly to Oregon and convince him to give himself up."

The superintendent didn't speak for a moment. Benjamin's existence, and everything else Micah had just revealed, was news to him.

"How long will you be gone?"

"A week at the most."

Dr. Hernandez stared at him. There couldn't be a worse time for Micah to disappear. Who else could refute the charges in Foster's letter? And who else could stand between the Board members who supported the school and the outraged voters who would believe Foster's claims?

"When are you leaving?" he asked.

"Monday morning."

"Call me every day that you're out of town."

"I'll try."

The old man set his jaw and glared at Micah.

"Every day, goddamn it!"

THIRTY-THREE.

As Friday dawned, Micah quickly dressed and skipped breakfast. Hamish's story would probably be in today's edition of the newspaper, and he was anxious to see it. When he backed the BMW down the driveway, its rear bumper barely missed a passing van he failed to spot in his eagerness to get on the road. Darting from lane to lane, he tried to break through the freeway's early morning congestion. But the other cars boxed him in.

A few blocks from the district's headquarters, he parked in front of a 7-11 store. Once he stepped through its double-wide glass doors, he froze in his tracks.

Before him was a stack of newspapers. In large capital letters across the top of the front page were these words:

SCHOOL SITE UNSAFE, STATE SAYS

He snatched the topmost copy. While other customers scurried around him to pay for their coffees and breakfast sandwiches, Micah stood under the store's harsh florescent lighting and scanned the article.

Two quotes startled him. The first was from Lee Grossman.

"The State certainly won't pay too much for a piece of property," the senator promised. "And we certainly won't purchase contaminated land."

The second was from Don Smith.

"The city has a responsibility to protect the health and safety of its citizens," the city manager proclaimed. "We may have to go to court to make sure the School Board doesn't do something irresponsible."

When Dr. Hernandez arrived, Micah was waiting outside his office. After he read the article, the old man pushed the newspaper away from him.

"Dealing with that"—he nodded towards the headline—"will be very tough for the Board members. Are you still leaving for Oregon on Monday?"

Micah returned his stare. "Yes, I am."

"This scheme of ours is about to blow up in the Board members' faces," the superintendent said. "And when it does, we'll have to find another site."

He lowered his head and clutched his hands together before him.

"It's been a morning for bad news," he said softly.

Raising his eyes, he looked at Micah.

"As I was leaving home, I got a call from Connie's husband. She passed away last night.

"It's sad enough that a fine woman is gone. But this also means the high school's in limbo—unless Violet or Jon decide to support the project. And I'm certainly not betting on that to happen."

Micah walked out of the superintendent's office and down the hallway in a daze. Connie's death wasn't a total surprise; the last time he saw her, the deterioration in her condition was startling. Nevertheless, it seemed as if his sorrow might suffocate him.

When he got outside, he paused for a moment and lowered his face. Their time together had been spent in anonymous hotel rooms, where their conversations were only brief interludes before and after their lovemaking. But hearing of her passing made him feel as though a part of himself had also died.

He raised his eyes to the sky.

"Shake it off," he whispered. "You don't have time to feel sorry for her. Or for yourself. There's plenty left to be done for the living."

Back at his desk, he called Sute and read aloud Grossman's quote.

"Lee knows Foster's letter isn't accurate," the big man said.

"But why would he imply Foster's on to something?"

"Calm down, my friend. Under the circumstances, what else could Lee say?"

"There has to be some way to take Foster out of the picture," Micah said.

"But how? He's the governor's boy."

Next, Micah called Judy. They hadn't spoken since their lunch at El Tapatio.

"Hey, stranger," he said.

"Is this my friend with the funny name? What's up?"

"Have you seen today's newspaper?"

She hesitated. "Yes, I have."

"It sounds like your boss is planning to sue us."

Judy didn't reply.

"Are you going to the Chamber mixer tonight?" he said.

"Yes. And you?"

"I'll be there."

Micah kept the receiver in his grasp as he dialed Sam Comstock's office.

"That was a rough story," the shopping center developer said. "Thank God you got three appraisals."

"Do you have some time this afternoon?"

"Sure. Want to meet at the bistro?"

"I'll see you there at four," Micah said.

The same elderly bartender was standing to the side of the liquor bottles when they arrived. He set the martinis in front of the pair before disappearing into the shadows.

Micah's voice broke the room's silence. "Having three appraisals won't be enough to close this deal."

Comstock met his stare with a frown.

"Because of Foster's letter, we're under more scrutiny than ever," he continued. "The Board members and the voters have to feel sure the district paid a fair price for the site."

Comstock narrowed his eyes. "What do you mean by a fair price?"

"Less than the amount in the appraisals."

"How much less?"

"Two million dollars less."

The businessman leaned back on the stool. "That's a hell of a lot of money."

Micah kept his eyes on Comstock.

"I need to prove you're not screwing us."

"I'll have to run this by my partners."

"That's fine," Micah said. "Just be sure to tell them you don't have a choice."

THIRTY-FOUR.

The Chamber of Commerce's annual City Mixer, a meet-and-greet cocktail reception, was held at the community's largest hotel. The nondescript building, which had opened to great fanfare a decade ago, was located a few blocks from the city hall and the county courthouse.

Micah arrived a half hour early and walked through the characterless lobby to the stark ballroom. He stopped at one of several portable bars that had been brought in for the event, ordered a drink and moved to a sofa.

Once he settled himself, Micah noticed Judy and Don Smith, standing together at the far side of the cavernous room. Smith looked like he was dressed for a luau; instead of his usual business suit, the city manager wore Bermuda shorts and a casual shirt splashed in loud colors.

Micah realized they were in the middle of a heated conversation. Judy was doing most of the talking. She moved her head up and down rapidly as she spoke. He heard the agitation in her voice, but couldn't make out her words.

While Micah looked on, Smith raised his arm and placed his hand on her shoulder as if to calm her. At that, she stepped backwards.

When he left his hand on her, she reached up and jerked it off. The pair glared at one another until Smith turned his back on her and stalked out a side door.

She stood motionless, staring in the direction of his departure. After a moment, she stepped over to the nearest bar. While she ordered a drink, Micah rose from the sofa and walked across the ballroom.

"Hello there."

Judy turned at the sound of his voice.

"Hello." A look of distress filled her dark eyes.

"Should we grab a seat?"

"All right."

He led her to the sofa.

"I saw that Don was here."

"He and his fishing buddies are on their way to Cabo for a long weekend. He only stopped by because I told him we needed to talk."

"What about?" he said.

"The lawsuit."

"Did he listen to you?"

"No," she said.

Neither spoke for a moment as they sipped their cocktails. Meanwhile, other guests began to drift into the room.

"I brought something for you," Micah said.

He reached into his coat's inside pocket, produced several folded pages and handed them to her. It was the Oregonian article about Benjamin.

When Judy finished reading the story, she looked at him, an expression of pained concern on her features.

"After Petersen faxed me that, I called the reporter who wrote it," Micah said. "She told me some things that make me think I have a chance of finding Benjamin. I'm flying to Portland on Monday."

"I can't tell you how glad I am to hear that." Judy glanced down at the fax again. "What is this name he calls himself? Welund."

"When Benjamin was a little boy, I used to take him to the library every Saturday morning. During one of our visits, I came across a book called Tales of the Vikings. It was full of Nordic legends: stories of mythological characters and their adventures. I'd check it out every few weeks and read the tales to Benjamin.

"His favorite was about a giant named Wada. The giant had a son named Welund. Even though he was only a boy, Wada decided he should learn a trade and apprenticed him to a renowned smith who made the finest swords in the land. But the smith mistreated Welund. When Wada learned of this, he traveled to the workshop and took the boy away.

"In order to return to their home, the pair had to cross a wide, deep river. There were no boats on the shore. So Wada lifted Welund onto his shoulder and waded through the waters to safety on the opposite bank."

Judy kept her eyes on him. "Benjamin's waiting for you to come and get him."

The ballroom was growing crowded now.

"How about another drink?" he said.

As he stood in line at the bar, Micah felt someone push roughly against his shoulder. He turned to face Comstock.

"How's it going, partner?" His speech was so slurred that his words ran together.

"I'm all right."

"And I've been sucking down martinis since you left me."

He stared purposefully into Micah's eyes.

"Can we find someplace to talk?"

"Judy's waiting for me to bring her a drink."

Comstock leaned forward until their noses were inches apart.

"Two million dollars. That's the biggest haircut anyone's ever given me."

Abruptly, he reached up with both hands and violently grasped the lapels of Micah's suit coat.

"What about being with me to hell and back...

"Partner?"

He literally spit out the word. Micah could feel the moisture of the spittle on his cheeks.

"Get your hands off me," he warned.

"Two million dollars," Comstock repeated despondently. The drunken anger had suddenly drained out of him. Now his eyes looked empty.

Because of the commotion, a crowd had gathered around them.

"You'd better get out of here and take a taxi home," Micah said, "before someone calls the cops."

Comstock let go of the coat. As he staggered away, he bumped into several of those who were watching.

When Micah returned to the sofa, Judy was no longer there. The room had filled. While he stood alone, a cocktail in each hand, Myron Richland appeared, squeezing his lanky frame between several other partygoers. With an amused look, the Board president glanced at the glasses in Micah's hands.

"You must be really thirsty," he quipped.

Micah stopped a server who was walking past and impatiently placed the drinks on her tray.

"Got a few minutes?" Richland said. "I need to talk over something with you."

Silently, Micah followed him across the ballroom and through an outside doorway. It led to an unlighted concrete courtyard. They were the only ones who stood in the shadows of the space.

"This afternoon, Betty Phelan told me the city attorney is preparing to file a lawsuit against the district," Richland said. "Do you realize what this would mean? A court battle between us and them will tear the community apart. Look at what's already happening at our Board meetings. We spend all our time listening to the school's proponents and opponents. It feels like this city is on the verge of a political civil war."

Richland placed his hands on his hips. "I know how great the need is for another high school. But this project has too much baggage—especially now that the State's claiming we want to purchase a contaminated piece of property that's overpriced."

"What will the voters think," Micah said, "if we don't build a high school?"

The Board president crossed his arms.

"I'll tell them our staff failed to find a site I could support. That you let me and the rest of the Board down."

At that moment, Dr. Hernandez emerged from the brightly lit ballroom and walked towards them. As he approached, Richland nodded towards Micah.

"We were talking about our favorite facility project."

Dr. Hernandez pursed his lips. "I've told him we may have to find another site."

Richland glanced at Micah. "I couldn't agree more."

"Shall we go inside?" the old man said.

Micah stood by himself on the patio and watched them disappear into the throng of corporate executives, business owners, politicians and bureaucrats. Except for the winter afternoon when his wife drew her last breath while he sat helplessly next to her hospital bed, he couldn't remember another point in his life when he'd felt so alone.

As he stared numbly at the crowd inside the ballroom, he spotted Judy. She was standing before a large window that faced the courtyard. Anxiously, he pushed his way through the anonymous bodies that separated them.

"I've been looking for you," she said.

"And I still owe you a drink."

After they found a bar, he took her hand and led her outside to the courtyard. They faced one another in the twilight. He raised his glass and tapped it lightly against hers, and they each took a long drink of the rum and Coke.

Judy stared at him.

"I'm in trouble," she said. "It's not good for someone's career to cross Don. I had to tell him what I thought about the lawsuit. I know he and the Council are wrong.

"But…this job means everything to me.

"Before my parents came to California, they lived in a shack without electricity or running water. They picked cotton from dawn until sundown. Because they left Jalisco, I've had the opportunity to get a graduate degree and take on an important career. The last thing I thought I'd ever do is endanger what we've accomplished.

"But I'm afraid that's exactly what I've done."

"My boss is upset with me, too," Micah said. "Since the letter came from the State, he's wondering if trying to build the high school is worth the heat the Board members are taking. And he blames me for the fix they're in.

"He told me I have to find another site. Except there aren't any."

Micah glanced at her empty glass. "Looks like you're ready for another drink. So am I."

He returned a few minutes later with the cocktails. They each drank deeply. Then she looked up at him.

"I told Don I've seen a different side of him." She had begun to slur her words. "A side that's willing to sacrifice the future of the city's kids to placate Betty and her supporters.

"A side that I despise."

She drew in a deep breath. "I can't believe I actually said that to him."

At that moment, her glass slipped out of her grip and shattered on the patio's surface. The spilled brown liquid, ice cubes and shards seemed to be everywhere.

"It's time for me to go home," she said. "Can you give me a ride? It's not far from here."

Most of those who had been in the ballroom were gone. The couple walked through the lobby and out of the building's front doors.

"Where do you live?" Micah asked as the BMW left the parking lot.

"Go north on Raymond Avenue."

He thought the rum had confused her. "You mean south?"

"No. North."

They drove past the glow of Fairview Plaza's neon business signs and pole lights. After a few blocks, she pointed to a street on their left. They entered the community's most upscale neighborhood; these were the streets Micah had driven after his first visit to the Plaza. They seemed very different at night. The only illumination came from an occasional street lamp and front porch light. On both sides of the narrow road, the mansions hulked anonymously in the darkness.

Where is she taking me? he asked himself.

At Judy's direction, they turned right and then left again. After the second turn, she pointed to the side of the road.

"Stop here."

They parked in front of an unlighted void that Micah assumed must be a lawn. Beyond it, the outline of the biggest house he had ever seen lurked at the top of a rise.

"Is this where you live?" he said.

"Quite a place, isn't it?"

He figured she must be pulling his leg. "I know the city pays its managers well. But this is ridiculous!"

"This is Don's house," she said.

He stiffened, staring at the silhouette of her face.

"He's a widower too. His wife died in a traffic accident a few years before he hired me." She spoke very slowly, trying to keep her thoughts straight through the haze of the alcohol.

"At first, our relationship was all about work. He showed me what it took to lead the city's departments and deal with the Council. And he gave me important projects to supervise. It was all very flattering, especially for someone my age.

"One day, he asked me to join him for lunch. That became a daily ritual. And then—"

"One thing led to another," he said.

Judy began to push awkwardly at the passenger door. He climbed out of the BMW, walked around the car and pulled the door open. Taking her hand, he helped her slip out of the seat and stand on the sidewalk. Patiently, he walked behind her, his hand on her shoulder, as she stepped unsteadily along the walkway that crossed the invisible lawn and led up the darkened rise.

While he watched, she unlocked the massive front door. Then she turned to him. "Call me when you get back from Oregon," she said.

Reaching up, she put one hand on each side of his face, pulled his head down to her and kissed him on the lips.

The tiny figure stepped into the house and disappeared. The door creaked loudly as she pushed it closed. Like a cell door sealing in a prisoner.

Micah became lost when he tried to find his way out of the neighborhood. After several minutes of driving in circles, he finally came across Raymond Avenue and turned south. When he reached the Plaza, he steered into the empty north parking lot. Shutting off the car's engine and lights, he began to walk the lot's perimeter. As he circled back, a pick-up truck appeared and pulled up beside him.

"What're you doing here?" the security guard asked him roughly.

"Nothing. Just stretching my legs."

"You don't belong here."

Micah stared at him. "You might be right."

"Hit the road."

The pick-up followed him, its high beams unbearably bright in his mirrors, as he drove across the parking lot and turned back onto Raymond Avenue.

THIRTY-FIVE.

On Saturday evening, Micah was to come by Denise's house to take her to dinner. He left his place while the sun was still above the western horizon. There were several stops he needed to make. Various construction projects were now underway across the district. Because of his hectic schedule, it was difficult to find the time to visit them during the week. Walking the sites this afternoon would give him a sense of each job's progress.

His first stop was the Grimm Farm Elementary project. As Officer Zavala had recommended after the vandalism by the gang members, a security guard now lived on the site; the contractor installed a travel trailer for his use next to the job office.

The guard, a wiry black man named Ned who wore a Dodgers baseball cap and had retired from the Marines a few years before, happened to be standing at the front of the property when Micah pulled up.

"I hear there haven't been any more problems since you moved in." As he spoke, Micah turned his head, studying the property. The school was made up of a collection of separate buildings that had been framed over the previous few weeks. Behind them stood the dilapidated farmhouse and barn, waiting for the improvements Micah had promised the Grimm sisters and Don Smith.

"It was louder than hell on the night of Cinco de Mayo, though," Ned said. "The folks in this neighborhood got their hands on some heavy ordnance." He slapped his open palm against his trim stomach and cackled. "I thought I was back in 'Nam!"

"Anyone ever come around here?"

"Oh, sure. Lots of parents bring their children by." Ned paused. "One of the gang members comes by, too."

"Is that right?"

"Yes sir. He's covered with prison tattoos. Even has 'em on his face."

Ned stared at Micah. "I asked if he was casing the place. He said 'Damn right.'"

"Think he was kidding?"

"He wasn't kidding. The contractor leaves lots of stuff here every night that they could hock or cash in at a recycling center."

Ned pulled on the bill of his cap. "He said they'd give me a cut of the take if I disappeared for a couple of hours. I won't repeat the four letter words I used when I answered him."

"Thank God we told the contractor to hire you."

The guard laughed again. "My thought exactly!"

Micah drove next to the motel's former location. Construction of the second elementary school was well underway. After that, he headed north on Raymond Avenue. He could see the traffic signal at Fairview Boulevard a half mile ahead when he turned east onto a two lane street that bisected a modest residential neighborhood.

On his right was James Madison Intermediate School, the campus where the district planned to remodel the auditorium. A large, windowless structure, it had been designed in the Bauhaus style, with curved corners and cubic details. Like the rest of the school, the auditorium was built in the 1930's by the Works Progress Administration, the New Deal agency established to create jobs during the Great Depression.

For the initial twenty years of its existence, Madison was used as a high school. When rapid and widespread residential development led to a drastic increase in the city's population during the 1950's, the district constructed two larger high school campuses to deal with the growing enrollment. Madison was converted to a school for seventh and eighth grade students.

In the evenings and on weekends, the auditorium hosted various events, including concerts by a professional symphony orchestra. The conductor told Micah the auditorium's acoustic qualities were far superior to those of the performing arts spaces at the two newer high schools.

"When you remodel that building, you better not screw it up," he said—only half-jokingly. Because of the conductor's comment, the district retained a specialist in designing professional concert halls to assist the project architect.

Micah didn't have a way to enter the locked auditorium. He drove slowly past it before making a U-turn on the quiet street.

Raymond Avenue Elementary was his last stop before reaching Denise's house. The new multi-purpose building stood half-completed. He made his way slowly through the structure, stepping over construction debris as he went. Then he walked between the portable classrooms and across the playfield until he reached the area where the parking lot would be constructed for the land saver school students.

Across the street was a row of large, well-kept houses. For the first time, he wondered how the neighbors would react when they learned about the new parking lot—and the teenagers who would be driving past their houses every day to use it.

Just what we need, he thought, shaking his head as he considered his lack of foresight. Even more pissed-off voters.

The sun disappeared while he returned to his car and turned north on Raymond Avenue. The homes of the city's aristocracy lined both sides of the boulevard. According to Denise's directions, he would be making a left turn at Dunbar Lane, a right turn onto McCall Place and another left turn at Shadburn Way, the street where she lived.

The Dunbar street sign appeared after only a few hundred feet. Micah sensed he had followed this route before. By the time he made the turn onto Shadburn, he realized he was approaching Don Smith's house.

Just ahead, a gigantic Mission Revival mansion loomed at the peak of a rise. He studied the place as he drove slowly past. There was no one in sight.

In another hundred yards, he arrived at Denise's residence, a sprawling two story Craftsman structure situated on a large corner parcel. He parked on the circular driveway that crossed the front of the property and walked up a stone stairway to the expansive front porch.

She answered the door, smiling warmly and looking radiant in a black dress that highlighted her attractive figure. Her modest use of make-up was refreshing; it reminded Micah of how self-assured she always seemed.

"The babysitter just arrived," she said. "I'm ready to go whenever you are."

Dinner was at one of the community's most distinctive restaurants. Both inside and out, the building replicated an English country inn. A young woman, dressed as an eighteenth century serving wench, led them through its faux pub interior to a corner booth.

"How was your week?" he said after they were seated.

"I'm playing in a tournament at my tennis club next month, so my coach and I have been practicing quite a bit." Her voice was full of enthusiasm. "I love the sport so much. Even practice is fun."

A server appeared at their table to take their beverage orders. Denise asked for sparkling water. Micah hesitated for a moment when he heard this. Then he called for an iced tea.

After the server disappeared, Micah asked: "Do you ever drink liquor?"

"No. I'm Mormon. I tried a shot of tequila once at a party when I was in college." She grinned sheepishly. "I was very sorry I did!"

She studied his face. "I don't need to ask how your week's gone. I saw the article in the newspaper."

"Because of the letter from the State," he said, "the Board members are worried that the voters have turned against them."

"Do you think they'll have the courage to build the school?"

He shook his head. "I don't know anymore."

They both ordered prime rib, the restaurant's specialty.

"Did I tell you that, next month, I'll become the new president of the PTA Council?" she said.

"Congratulations." He raised his glass and tapped it against hers. "That'll keep you busier than ever."

She nodded. "We're going to start a student recipe contest to encourage healthy eating. And Read Across America Day is just a few weeks away. Janelle and Janice's classmates are coming over. I'll make some hot chocolate and we'll read to each other."

"The PTA is a wonderful organization," he said. "And it's made up of some wonderful people."

She smiled his way.

Soon, their dinners arrived. Micah watched Denise as she cut into the slab of beef. "Speaking of your kids...Has it been tough raising them on your own?"

"Not really. A woman comes in every afternoon to keep the house in order and prepare dinner. And Jack, my ex-husband, takes them for a few days each month."

"What happened between you two?" he said.

She put down her fork. "Being a husband and father aren't Jack's priorities. He's a workaholic. During our marriage, he was never home, or at the kids' activities. I was already raising them by myself.

"That's not only being a poor father. It's a betrayal of our faith. We believe family should be at the center of our lives."

Micah glanced down at the glass of iced tea. Hearing about the failings of another inadequate father gave him the urge for something much stronger.

"I'll be right back," he said, putting aside his napkin.

He walked into the bar and stopped in front of the rows of liquor bottles. Downing a shot of bourbon would take no time at all. She'd assume he had been to the restroom. But she might smell the booze on his breath. He raised one hand and rubbed his open palm nervously along the side of his face as he stood there. Then he returned to Denise.

"Have you ever thought about becoming more involved at the district?" he asked.

"You mean, besides the PTA? What else did you have in mind?"

"Running for the Board," he said.

Her eyes widened. "No. I never have." She continued to watch him. "It's an interesting idea, though."

"You'd be an excellent member. You're thoughtful and involved. And you'd help the rest of the Board to see issues from a parent's perspective. Phil is the only one of them who has kids in our schools.

"Do you think Jack would help with your campaign?"

"Probably. Since the divorce, we actually get along better than we have in years. He certainly knows a lot about winning elections.

"Speaking of the Board," she said, "did you hear that Connie passed away?"

He nodded.

"Everyone knew she was ill. I had no idea, though, that her condition was so serious. What was wrong with her?"

"It's a mystery. She'd seen numerous doctors, but no one could get to the bottom of it."

Denise moved her face closer to his and lowered her voice.

"One afternoon a few weeks ago, I was helping out at the school and went outside to get something from my station wagon. Someone had placed a flyer about Connie on the windshields of every car in the lot. It claimed she was having affairs with men who worked at the district.

"Why would someone want to spread an ugly rumor like that?" she said. "Who do you think would do such a thing?"

He lowered his eyes and shook his head.

As he drove Denise back home, they passed Fairview Plaza.

"Do you really think the Board might give up on the new school?" she said.

He glanced at her. "I do."

They passed Smith's mansion and he parked the BMW in front of Denise's house.

"I'm glad you finally asked me to dinner," she said as they sat in the dark.

"Should we do it again?"

"You'd better ask me out again, or you'll be in trouble."

He took her hand in his. "I certainly don't want any trouble."

"I didn't think you would."

"Next week, I'm going out of town. I'll call you when I get back."

Neither of them spoke for a moment. The neighborhood was so quiet that he could hear her breathing.

"You asked if the Board might abandon the school," he said. "You can stop that from happening.

"The Board won't approve the project until Fred Foster's claims are disproven. He's a political appointee who was placed in his position by the governor's office. That means the governor's office can send a new letter to the district that refutes everything Foster's written."

"Should my ex talk to the governor?"

He squeezed her hand. "Tell Jack what's at stake: saving the school his children will attend some day."

"I'll take care of it. That's the least I can do, after you've gotten it this far on your own."

He walked her up the lighted stairway to the front door. As they stood on the porch, he grasped her slim waist and pulled her to him.

While they kissed, slowly and deeply, he felt her hands, caressing the back of his neck.

"Don't forget to call me," she said as they held one another.

He pressed his cheek against hers.

"I won't," he whispered.

THIRTY-SIX.

While Micah spent Saturday afternoon visiting the construction projects, his son was on the run from the Astoria Police Department.

Since the Oregonian article appeared, the local law enforcement agencies had redoubled their efforts to find him. In the rural areas with the vacation houses, police and sheriff's cruisers were now everywhere.

He began to spend more of the daylight hours in Astoria. Here, he could blend in with the other teenage runaways who panhandled on its streets and slept on the stoops and in the alleys of its decaying downtown.

But Benjamin never stayed overnight in the city. At dusk, he'd board a public transit bus and ride to Astoria's sparsely populated outskirts. Under cover of darkness, he wandered the forested hillocks until he found a dwelling without any lights.

The previous evening, the teenager broke into a mansion with a "For Lease" sign stuck in the front lawn. In the huge living room, there was a row of picture windows facing towards the northwest. The lights of the Astoria-Megler Bridge looked like a string of diamonds as the span crossed the Columbia River, invisible in the blackness.

Benjamin lay down on the plush carpet that covered the floor in front of the window and fell asleep.

At dawn, he awoke and began rummaging through the mansion. Even though he found very little of value in the empty house, his search still took several hours.

On the verge of leaving, he pulled open one last door—and found a vintage Mercedes coupe parked in the garage. Earlier, he came across the car's ignition key, hanging on a hook in the kitchen's pantry.

He decided to try and start the Mercedes.

Using a crow bar, he broke the lock that secured the garage's wide double wooden doors and swung them open. When he slipped behind the steering wheel and turned the key in the ignition, the engine turned over and, without hesitation, rumbled to life.

He ground the gears several times before realizing how to get the shifter at his side into reverse. As he touched the gas pedal lightly with his right foot, the low, streamlined vehicle jerked backwards.

This isn't so hard, he thought. I'll have it figured out in a couple of minutes.

He had navigated numerous stolen watercraft across the wild and unpredictable Columbia—and several times, barely survived the experience. As Petersen told Micah, the river was one of the most treacherous in the world.

This afternoon, Benjamin intended to make the crossing over the Astoria-Megler Bridge.

I should've thought of this before. Driving a car to the Washington side is much safer than sailing over, he told himself.

What he didn't grasp was the fact that this particular car would attract plenty of attention. The Mercedes was a 1955 300 SL, famous for the way its doors opened by rising out and above the car's roofline. This feature had earned the coupe its nick-name—"gullwing."

Benjamin was behind the wheel of one of the rarest and most expensive cars in the world.

Cautiously now, he backed the coupe out of the garage, got it into first gear and steered it slowly down the mansion's long, steep driveway. Once he turned onto the empty country road, the teenager pushed down on the gas pedal. The Mercedes jumped forward, its loud, sharp exhaust note echoing through the forest that lined both sides of the street. The pine trees and mailboxes began to rush by him.

He glanced at the dashboard. The speedometer read ninety-two miles per hour.

At the bottom of the hill, he reached the Columbia River Highway and turned the silver sports car west towards Astoria and the bridge. The road followed the shoreline, passing several large warehouses as well as heavy engine repair shops and other businesses that served those who made their living on the river. Beyond the buildings, a dozen or more enormous cargo ships were anchored in the Columbia's channel.

It only took a few minutes before Benjamin spotted the first police car, traveling in the opposite direction on the highway. Once it passed, he could see in his rearview mirrors that the black Dodge cruiser was making an abrupt U-turn in the middle of the road.

Someone must've stopped by the house after I left and called the cops, he thought.

Several vehicles separated him from the pursuing police car as the highway became Marine Avenue and entered Astoria's compact downtown. Just ahead, a second cruiser with "Astoria Police" stenciled on its side pulled up to a traffic signal and waited for the light to turn green as he passed through the intersection.

He had almost reached the ramp to the bridge. The span's hulking metal frame towered over the street ahead of him as it rose in the cloud-covered sky.

But he would be trapped if he drove onto the bridge.

Two police cruisers behind him

And across the river, the Pacific County sheriff's department

Surely waiting for him.

On Benjamin's right was a McDonald's and, just past it, a narrow side street. The teenager abruptly swerved onto the street and followed it to a parking lot at the rear of the restaurant. He squeezed the low-profile Mercedes behind a panel van and held his breath.

The McDonald's building blocked the policemen's view of Benjamin's madcap maneuver. They passed the restaurant and kept racing west on the avenue.

After a few minutes, he realized he had lost the cruisers. Since driving the coupe any further was out of the question, he raised its distinctive door and pulled himself out from behind the wheel. Crossing the parking lot, he walked towards the river. The street ended near the waterline, next to one of the bridge's massive steel support members.

Benjamin followed the sandy, trash-strewn shore under the bridge. As he emerged on the other side, he saw an old pier, jutting out into the Columbia's waters. Several boarded-up wooden buildings stood on its pilings. They had been constructed at the turn of the century to serve the Cooperative Packing Company, an enterprise established by union fishermen as the result of a labor dispute with the established canneries.

Past the pier, a veritable grove of sailboat masts lined the opposite side of a boulder-strewn breakwater. He was approaching the West Mooring Basin, a marina with four hundred boat slips.

Benjamin knew the marina's pedestrian entrance was on the far side; he had used it several times before. A handful of boat owners stood near the harbor master's office. They ignored him as the teenager walked past and entered the maze of docks where the various watercraft were tied up.

He picked one dock and began walking slowly on its timbered surface.

After several minutes, he stopped. Ahead was a MasterCraft Pro Star 190. The twenty foot long ski boat had an open cockpit and only one seat, in front of the steering wheel. Across its stern was painted the word WINGELOCK.

Alerts had been posted on the bulletin boards of the marinas along the river, detailing the rash of boat thefts Benjamin was responsible for committing. They warned owners to keep their ignition keys with them.

But old habits die hard; as Benjamin stood next to the Pro Star and looked down at the instrument panel, he saw that the key was in the ignition.

He stepped down into the craft.

Months before, during the midnight burglary of Hammonton's only hardware store, he took a copy of a thick book called Chapman Piloting & Seamanship. Known as the Bible of boating, it has been the leading reference work for boaters for almost one hundred years.

Studying the book provided him with the basics of operating a watercraft—and enough information to begin his wave of boat thefts.

Benjamin picked up an orange lifejacket laying at his feet, slipped it over his shoulders and tightened its straps. He turned the blower on to vent the engine box behind him of any combustible fumes. Then he primed the cold engine and tried to start it.

On the first attempt, it stuttered and stalled.

After he primed it again and engaged the starter, the engine burbled to life. The teenager hopped out of the boat, untied the bow and stern lines and got back behind the wheel. He pushed the throttle knob and the Pro Star began to move forward.

Several of those who sat in folding chairs on the decks of their boats waved to him while Benjamin slowly navigated past and towards the open river. To his right loomed the bridge, reflecting the light of the sinking sun as he exited the marina.

He planned to follow the Oregon coastline as it slanted northwest from Astoria and then cross the Columbia at its narrowest point. This section of the river was known to be dangerous and unpredictable, part of the infamous Columbia Bar. But that notorious reputation made it unlikely any law enforcement vessels would attempt to pursue him.

For now, the river was calm. In the distance, Benjamin could see a line of container ships, freighters and tankers moving upstream. The river's presence allowed Portland, which was seventy miles from the Pacific, to serve as an ocean port.

Following the shoreline, the ski boat drew closer to the river's mouth. The Columbia's flow began to clash with the incoming ocean current as both tried to get over the shallow bar at the same time.

The teenager could feel a wind coming up from the west. It blew harder and the serenity of the river rapidly disappeared, replaced within a few minutes by a series of breakers that increased in violence and size before Benjamin's eyes.

He steered the boat so it would strike the waves at a forty-five degree angle. According to Chapman, this course might prevent the craft from capsizing.

The sun disappeared beneath the ocean while the Pro Star passed between two red buoys and out into the channel. Now the breakers grew even larger and more treacherous, swirling unpredictably and forming whirlpools.

These were the worst conditions Benjamin had ever experienced. He pushed the throttle knob, increasing the craft's speed. It climbed a breaker and sailed through the air before crashing into another wave. He could barely control the boat. But the teenager maintained its rapid speed.

He was terrified—and desperate to reach the Washington side of the Columbia as soon as possible.

Up ahead, the Cape Disappointment Lighthouse's powerful beam sliced through the night while, along the shoreline, stationary green and red directional lights blinked methodically. Early in the century, a long wooden jetty had been constructed that protruded like a giant cactus spine into the river. The green light stood at the jetty's point, next to the mouth of a channel.

Even though the bar's violent waters continued to pound the Pro Star, Benjamin slowed the boat's speed. He had to be certain not to miss the channel. Otherwise, the wild river would send the small craft crashing into the rocky shore.

Seconds after he passed the light, a massive breaker abruptly slammed into the side of the boat, throwing it out of the shallow waterway and onto a pocket beach

Benjamin shut off the engine. The wind howled uncontrollably, raising a sound like that of a thousand coyotes stalking him in the darkness. But he was finally out of the Columbia's grasp.

After climbing unsteadily from the grounded craft, he stumbled for several steps before slumping onto the sand. His body trembled from the trauma of the crossing.

As he huddled on the beach, Benjamin grasped a medal that hung by a thin chain from his neck. He pressed it against his chest.

"When are you coming?"

He shouted

Breathlessly

Into the gale.

Goddamn it

When are you

Coming?

THIRTY-SEVEN.

Micah's flight landed at noon. He picked up a rental car and began the drive through Portland and its suburbs. Finally he was on his way to Astoria. For two hours, he followed the course of the Columbia River. As he approached his destination, he traveled the same highway into the town that Benjamin had taken in the stolen Mercedes coupe.

His hotel was an older, nondescript three story structure. When he walked from his car towards the entrance, Micah passed a teenager who was squatting on the sidewalk, a small plastic bowl in front of him with several dollar bills and some change. The young man had long, matted brown hair and wore a stained plaid shirt and torn blue jeans. Micah tried to study his sunburned features as he leaned down to place a dollar into the bowl, but the silent figure kept his eyes downturned.

I haven't seen Benjamin in four years, he told himself as he stared at the panhandler. I wonder if I'll recognize him.

After he checked in, went to his room and dropped off his bag, Micah took the elevator back down to the lobby. There was a display of brochures for various local points of interest against one wall. He stood before it for a moment until he found a pamphlet about the Fort Clatsop National Memorial. It included a map showing the fort's location in relation to Astoria and the region's road system.

When he stepped outside with the pamphlet in his hand, the teenager was gone. He aimed the rental car, a Chevrolet sedan, towards Marine Avenue and turned to the west. Once again, he was unknowingly following Benjamin's path from two days before; the Astoria-Megler Bridge's massive steel skeleton towered above him as he drove past the McDonald's, the cannery pier and the West Mooring Basin.

Now the road left Astoria and crossed a large bay. Past the opposite shoreline, Micah saw a turnoff for the town of Hammonton. He drove by it.

The highway entered a forest of big pines and spruce trees. He soon came to a sign that marked the road to Fort Clatsop. It ended at a parking lot that was almost empty; only one other vehicle was in sight, a dented VW Beetle with a brightly colored "Clinton/Gore 92" sticker on its rusted rear bumper.

At the edge of the lot, seven young people sat crosslegged in a half-circle on the sidewalk. Micah could hear a voice raised in song and the strumming of an acoustic guitar. As he approached, several of the teenagers turned their heads and stared. They were dressed in tatters like the panhandler he saw in Astoria.

A girl at the center of the group with thick, long hair dyed a striking bluish-green hue was playing a guitar and singing one of U2's ballads. She had a beautiful alto voice. In front of her set an open guitar case with random dollar bills and coins scattered inside.

As she finished the last line of the song, Micah bent down and placed a ten dollar bill in the case. The singer, whose aqua hair fell over her shoulders in a tangle, looked up.

"Thank you," she said stiffly.

"You're welcome."

He turned his gaze from her to the faces of the others.

"I'm here to ask for your help," he announced. "My name is Micah Wada. I'm looking for someone.

"Do any of you know Welund?"

Several of the teenagers glanced at one another, and the singer raised her amber eyebrows.

"No!"

A young man at the edge of the group with long black hair glared at Micah.

"Who are you, anyway?" he said indignantly. "A cop?"

"I'm not a cop. I'm Welund's father."

At that moment, a loud, clear ringing interrupted him. It was coming from a public phone mounted on a metal pole at the edge of the parking lot, twenty feet behind the young people. One of the teenagers jumped to his feet, walked briskly along the sidewalk to the phone and picked up the receiver.

Meanwhile, the rest of the group stared silently at him.

"I'll be here again tomorrow, if you have anything to tell me." Micah pointed at the pay phone. "If you'd rather call me, I'm staying at the Norseman Hotel in Astoria."

He turned his back on them. Ahead of him, a small free-standing sign with the word "FORT" stood along a gravel trail that led into the forest. Once he was out of sight among the trees and brush, Micah looked back towards the parking lot. The young man who had answered the phone was talking excitedly to the singer.

He continued following the trail. In a few minutes, he reached the site of Fort Clatsop. This was where the members of the Lewis and Clark expedition spent a miserable three months during the winter of 1805-1806. In the 1950's, a group of volunteers constructed a replica of the original fort on the site. Two long, narrow log buildings faced one another; stockades at each end of the fort secured the gaps between the structures.

A pair of open gates were located in the stockade nearest to Micah. Standing to the side of the entrance was a tall, heavy-set man in his late fifties who seemed to have stepped out of a time machine. He was dressed in a buckskin frock coat and pants and wore moccasins. Wrapped around his long gray hair was a black headscarf.

"Welcome to Fort Clatsop!" the man said. He stepped forward, a wide smile filling his bearded face, and shook Micah's hand. "My name's Frank Donaldson."

The docent proceeded to walk Micah through the fort. This took all of ten minutes.

"Have any questions?" he said after they returned to the gateway.

"There's a group of teenagers out by the parking lot. Where'd they come from?"

Donaldson's smile abruptly disappeared.

"They're from all over the northwest and beyond, and they have some sad tales to tell. They've run away from what passed for their families."

"What are they doing out here?"

"The tourists give them money. A free shuttle runs between the fort and Astoria, so it's easy for the kids to make the trip."

"While I was talking with them, the pay phone rang. One of the boys rushed over to answer it like he was expecting a call."

"That phone's what you might call their jungle drums," Donaldson said. "They use it to stay in touch with other runaways in Hammonton and Astoria and across the river."

Micah hesitated. "I read a story last week in the Oregonian about someone called Welund. Have you heard of him?"

"He's the kid who's stolen all the boats. Around here, he's something of a living legend."

"Does he ever come to the fort?"

The docent met his gaze. "I couldn't say. It's funny you ask me that, though. The chief of the Hammonton Police Department stopped by a few months back and asked me the same thing."

He fixed his eyes on Micah. "That cop was talking to the wrong guy. Those young people have already had enough hard times. I'm not going to help send one of them to prison."

Silently, he turned from Micah and walked through the gateway, disappearing into the fort.

The teenagers were still huddled together. Micah walked silently past them to the rental car, drove to the highway and turned towards Astoria. Instead of following the road across the bay, he took the Hammonton turnoff.

The town was nothing more than a collection of modest storefronts clustered on both sides of the road. As he drove slowly by, he saw a sign pointing down a side street with "COLUMBIA MARINA" painted on it and, half a mile later, a second directional sign on the opposite side of the road that read Hammonton Police Department.

He kept driving north. After a few minutes, he reached Fort Stevens State Park, a nature preserve at the end of the peninsula. Micah meandered through the park until he came upon an isolated parking lot. Next to it was a concrete viewing platform at the edge of the water.

This was the shoreline Benjamin had been following before he began his crossing of the river.

Standing there, Micah grasped for the first time the Columbia's size and power. Even though he gazed across one of the river's narrowest points, the opposite shore in Washington state was still several miles in the distance. Millions of gallons of water rushed past him, moving towards the bar and the ocean. Its roar was deafening.

When he returned to the hotel and parked the car, Micah didn't go to his room but walked to a building a few blocks away. He had an appointment with an attorney named Patrick Kelly.

In his late thirties, Kelly was a chubby man of medium height with a full head of brown hair. They sat across from one another at a small round table in the attorney's office.

Over the phone, the pair had discussed Benjamin's situation several times.

"Go over the legal process again after he's arrested," Micah said.

"To make a long story short, it would begin with an arraignment, when he's advised of the charges. At that time, a preliminary hearing gets scheduled. Once probable cause is found at the hearing, we enter a plea and the judge sets a trial date."

"Any chance we could negotiate a plea agreement?"

Kelly frowned. "It's not likely. These crimes were not of a violent nature. But there were dozens of them—and they created fear throughout the community."

He watched Micah. "I started locking my house every morning when I left for work; I'd never done that before.

"Also, the value of the items taken adds up to a huge amount of money. It's fortunate the authorities have been able to return most of the costliest items—the boats—to their owners. But folks around here are very upset about all of this. They want their pound of flesh. And the prosecutors represent the people."

"If Benjamin is found guilty, what would his sentence likely be?"

"It depends on the charges and the strength of the evidence."

"Give me the worst-case scenario," Micah said.

"Worst case?" Kelly repeated. "Seven to ten years in state prison. Although, with credit for good behavior, he might serve only half that time."

Micah felt as though he had been punched in the stomach.

"My God!" The anger in his voice startled the attorney. "My son's been homeless since he was fourteen. And now you're telling me he might be locked up until he's almost thirty years old."

"The legal system and the defense I can mount will determine that. Don't forget—it's also possible he'll be found not guilty, or receive a lesser sentence.

"But there's little doubt he'll face charges at some point. The law enforcement agencies in this part of the Northwest send all the fingerprints they've collected at crime scenes to the FBI's database in Washington, D.C. If your son is fingerprinted in the future, even if it's years from now and a thousand miles from here, the agency that submitted the prints to the FBI will be notified."

"Notified of what?" Micah said.

"That the prints belong to a suspected felon. And a fugitive from the law."

THIRTY-EIGHT.

The next morning, Micah saw a stack of newspapers on the hotel lobby's front desk. It was that day's edition of the Oregonian. He grabbed a copy and walked a block to a diner he had spotted the day before. Every table in the small restaurant was occupied, so he sat on a stool at the counter.

After he took a few sips of his coffee, Micah opened the Oregonian's front page.

A headline at the bottom of the page startled him.

Is Sailing Thief Sunk? it asked.

"The Astoria region's infamous 'sailing thief' has apparently struck again," the article began. "But he may have pulled off his final boat heist.

"On Sunday morning, the captain of a fishing trawler returning to Baker Bay reported an abandoned ski boat along the Washington state shoreline. According to the Astoria Police Department, the boat was stolen on Saturday evening from the West Mooring Basin at the foot of the Astoria-Megler Bridge.

"'Whoever it is that took the boat would have been very fortunate to make it across the Columbia Bar that night,' said Commander Franklin Furst, a spokesman for the Coast Guard station at Cape Disappointment. 'He may have been swept into the river before the boat was beached. That's how treacherous the conditions were.'

"The ski boat heist bears the hallmarks of the 'sailing thief', the teenage runaway from Southern California who has admitted to a string of watercraft thefts and burglaries over the last several years. Two other boats have also been taken from the West Mooring Basin in the last 18 months.

"'It sounds like this young criminal is at it again,' noted Pacific County sheriff Hugh Dervish. 'But he was taking quite a chance, going out on the bar in high seas with a strong wind blowing in from the Pacific. If he keeps this up, he'll drown before we catch up with him. For all we know, he may have drowned on Saturday night.'

"On Saturday afternoon, a rare Mercedes 'gullwing' coupe was stolen from a residence to the southeast of Astoria. It was found abandoned in a parking lot near the marina where the ski boat was taken. Astoria police are investigating a possible link between the two crimes."

Micah folded the newspaper and set it down. Then he placed his elbows on the counter top and covered his face with his hands.

In the late morning, he drove to Fort Clatsop again. The teenagers squatted on the sidewalk. It was as though they hadn't moved since he saw them the previous afternoon. He walked across the parking lot and once again stopped before them.

"I don't know if you've heard what my son did on Saturday night." There was a tremor in his voice. "He took a stolen boat across the Columbia Bar in the worst possible conditions.

"If he stays on the run, he's going to drown, or else a cop will kill him. Either way, it'll be senseless."

The girl with the blue-green hair was watching him.

"Are you going to help me?" he said.

No one answered.

Micah stood there a moment longer, staring at the runaways. Then he began walking slowly back towards the Chevrolet.

The sound of footsteps on the asphalt caused him to turn. The girl was standing next to him, slender and very tall. A cluster of freckles covered her cheeks and nose.

"Can you give me a lift?"

He nodded.

"I need to see your driver's license first," she said.

Pulling out his wallet, he handed the license to the teenager. She studied both sides of the card, turning it in the sunlight.

"Okay," she muttered, handing it back to him.

"What's your name?" he said as the car passed the other teenagers.

"Tranquility."

"Where are we going?"

"Drive to Astoria."

They pulled onto the highway.

"Did you grow up around here?" he said.

"No. In Colorado."

"What brought you to Oregon?"

"My mom and dad divorced a while back." She spoke in a monotone. "About two years ago, she met a guy and got married again. Whenever she wasn't around, he'd come on to me. I finally got fed up and told her. She called me a homewrecker and threw me out." She kept her eyes on the road ahead. "I met some kids when I was hitchhiking who were headed this way. So I came with them."

They crossed the bay and approached downtown Astoria.

"Get on the big bridge," she said.

He drove up a steep, curving ramp to the start of the Astoria-Megler Bridge. It towered two hundred feet above the river's surface, providing an expansive vista of the waterway and the surrounding countryside.

"How did you learn to sing so well?"

She shrugged. "I used to harmonize with CDs in my bedroom."

When you still had a bedroom, he thought.

"Are you Benjamin's girlfriend?"

"Benjamin?"

"I mean Welund. Are you his girlfriend?" he asked again.

She hesitated. "Sort of."

They had almost reached the end of the bridge. Ahead of them was a treeless shoreline and a fork in the highway.

"Go to the left," she said.

He noticed she was clutching a scrap of paper with handwritten directions on it. He recognized the large block letters.

Following the edge of Baker Bay, the highway passed through several tiny fishing villages. Soon, they entered the little town of Ilwaco.

She told him to make a right turn. After several miles, the pavement ended but the road continued, covered now with gravel. They were in a forested area with few buildings.

"We're looking for number two-three-one," she said.

It was at the end of the road: a small house, looking unkempt and possibly abandoned. Square windows with crinkled, dusty blinds framed the flaking wooden door.

Tranquility got out of the car and, without a word, began walking back down the road towards the town.

"Where are you going?" he called out.

She ignored him.

He turned back to the house. The door had opened. Standing in the opening was a lanky teenager with shoulder-length sand colored hair.

Micah stepped towards the figure until they were only a few feet apart. Father and son did not look at all alike. Benjamin had azure eyes, a narrow face and angular nose.

"I'd forgotten how much you resemble your mother," Micah said quietly as they stared at one another. He extended his right arm.

Benjamin hesitated. Then he took Micah's hand and shook it quickly, in a jerking motion, like someone who is new to the practice.

"Welcome to my hideout." His voice sounded much like his father's, strong and clear.

Once Micah followed him inside, Benjamin closed the door and locked it. The cramped and musty smelling room held too many pieces of old, mismatched furniture. Because of the blinds that covered the windows, a lamp on a corner table provided the only illumination.

"Have a seat." Benjamin pointed towards a large chair. He sat in a smaller one across from his father.

"I can't tell you how happy I am to see you," Micah said.

The teenager watched him for a moment.

"I've been thinking about this day for a long time." He paused again. "I used to hate you. After Mom got sick and passed away, I was sure you didn't want me anymore."

"I know." Micah remembered the note Benjamin taped on the BMW's windshield before he disappeared.

YOU ARE THE MOST SELFISH ASSHOLE IN THE WORLD. YOU ABANDONED ME A LONG TIME AGO. NOW I AM ABANDONING YOU.

"I've already hired an attorney. I'm going to do whatever it takes to get all of this straightened out."

"Someone showed me a newspaper article that said I'll have to go to prison for ten years," Benjamin said.

They stared at one another.

"Speaking of newspaper stories," Micah said, "I read one this morning about a ski boat that was found beached on the Washington shoreline. Someone took it from a marina and tried to cross the bar in very rough conditions."

Without a word, Benjamin stood and stepped through an open doorway next to Micah's chair. When he reappeared, he held the bright orange lifejacket with WINGELOCK stenciled across its back. He dropped the jacket at Micah's feet.

"I didn't think I was going to make it," he said. "The river tossed the boat around like a toy in a bathtub. After it was forced onto the shore, I walked all the way here without realizing I still had the jacket on. That's how shaken up I was."

"The Coast Guard and sheriff seem to think whoever took the boat was swept into the river and drowned," Micah said.

"The cops would call off their manhunt if they thought you were dead."

Benjamin tilted his head.

"They'll be looking for proof you were thrown into the Columbia. What if we give them a hand by dumping some of your stuff into the river?"

"Sounds like a plan!" Benjamin replied gleefully.

Micah looked down and set the end of his shoe on the lifejacket.

"Here's something we can use. What else do you have?"

Once again, Benjamin disappeared. When he returned, he handed a stack of credit cards to his father. As he flipped through them, Micah saw they had been issued by a variety of financial institutions. The name of the account holder was different on each.

"You have quite a collection here."

"A lot of people leave them laying around their houses." Benjamin shook his head. "It surprised the heck out of me."

"Don't the sales clerks ask for your ID?"

"I order things over the phone and have them shipped to the houses where I stole the cards."

"What sorts of things?"

Benjamin shrugged. "All kinds of stuff."

Micah glanced at the boy's blue jeans and plaid shirt. His son's clothes were not worn out like those of the other runaways.

"Have anything else we can throw in the river?"

The teenager raised both hands to the back of his neck and unfastened a thin chain. A Saint Christopher medal dangled from it.

"Remember this?" he said, holding the medallion in front of Micah's face.

Benjamin's parents gave it to him on his twelfth birthday. Its reverse side displayed the following inscription:

> To Our Beloved Son
> Be Always Safe As You
> Journey Through Life

Six months after Benjamin's mother read it aloud and fastened the chain around his neck, her journey ended.

Micah abruptly got to his feet and reached for his son. They embraced so tightly that he felt himself coming up short of breath. But he didn't want his boy to let him go.

With the lifejacket tucked under his arm and the credit cards and Saint Christopher medal in his pocket, Benjamin followed Micah out to the Chevrolet. They took the highway south to Cape Disappointment State Park. Before them stood the lighthouse. Since the nineteenth century, the powerful beam that glimmered from the top of the tall, round, whitewashed structure had been guiding ships to the Columbia's mouth.

Micah parked in a lot below the lighthouse. Leaving the lifejacket in the car, they hiked to the top of a bluff. From here, Benjamin pointed out the long jetty with the directional light at its tip and the narrow beach below them where the ski boat was flung ashore. The authorities had already towed it away. The pair followed the clifftop until they had almost reached the lighthouse. It nestled on a wooded point above the bar.

Along the shoreline, just to the northwest, they could see a small inlet with a sandy beach.

"If we drop the stuff into the river here," Benjamin said, "it'll wash up on that beach and be easy to find." He nodded towards a path ahead of them. "There's a trail I could take down to the water."

"Good idea." Micah looked back at the parking lot, which was almost full. "Except there's too many people around."

They stopped at a roadside stand to pick up a couple of hamburgers and returned to the little house. The pair sat in the small, shadowy living room, nibbling on the sandwiches and sipping from bottles of Coke. It dawned on Micah that he couldn't remember the last time they had eaten a meal together.

At sunset, they returned to Cape Disappointment. Now there were only a few cars. The lighthouse's brilliant band of light flashed above their heads. Benjamin led the way, holding a flashlight in one hand and the lifejacket in the other, as they retraced their path from that afternoon. At the head of the trail, they stopped.

"Hang on to the medallion and some of the credit cards," Micah said.

"Why?"

"You'll find out."

Benjamin descended the bluff and disappeared.

After a few minutes, Micah spotted the flashlight's beam, bobbing up and down with each of Benjamin's steps as he scaled the steep trail back to the clifftop. They walked quickly to the Chevrolet and drove away. Micah didn't turn on the car's headlights until they left the parking lot.

"How'd it go?" he said.

"The current's carrying the cards and lifejacket downriver. Just like we planned."

Micah steered the car through the center of Ilwaco and continued on as the road circled Baker Bay and headed towards the Astoria-Megler Bridge. At the point where the bridge began to rise above the Washington shoreline, he pulled over.

"Dump the rest of the credit cards in the river," he said, nodding towards the guardrail.

"What about the Saint Christopher medal?"

"Your mother would want you to keep it."

They stared at one another. Then Benjamin got out and flung the handful of remaining credit cards over the railing. Like haunted confetti, the plastic rectangles fluttered towards the water in the dim light of the quarter-moon that had just risen.

While the car crossed the Columbia, Micah glanced at his son. Memories of long-past afternoons flashed across his mind. Afternoons spent reading aloud the tale of Wada and Welund as Benjamin sat at his knee.

When they reached Astoria, Micah drove to the hotel. He went to his room, threw his belongings into his bag and checked out. Once he slipped back into the Chevrolet, Benjamin asked: "Where are we going?"

"The Portland Airport."

The countryside along the highway was anonymous, hidden by the night. Only the sparse lights of an occasional small town interrupted the monotony. After ninety minutes or so, the car began to pass through the ugly urban sprawl of Portland's suburbs.

"We want the police to think I was by myself," Micah said. "If they find out I wasn't alone, they'll assume you flew to Southern California with me."

He pulled out his wallet and handed it to Benjamin. "Take two hundred dollars."

His son slipped the bills into his shirt pocket.

"I'm going to drop you off at the front of the terminal. Use the cash to purchase a ticket for the next flight to L.A. If anyone asks questions, tell them you're going to visit your grandfather. Just remember—we can't let others see that we know each other."

They were part of the last group of passengers to board the jet. Benjamin entered the plane first and found his seat at the cabin's midpoint. Micah kept his eyes forward as he shuffled down the aisle to the rear of the aircraft.

When the plane climbed into the sky, he leaned back in his seat and heaved a sigh of relief. Then he began to consider what might happen during the next several weeks.

Hopefully, the authorities would find the credit cards and lifejacket. In the meantime, they would also see that the wave of burglaries and boat thefts had ended. This chain of events could be enough to assure them that Benjamin had drowned.

Micah assumed they'd learn of his visit to the Astoria region. If investigators contacted him, he would tell them he had been unable to find Benjamin. In fact, he hadn't arrived in Oregon until two days after the teenager's fateful attempt to cross the Columbia Bar.

But if someone happened to admit hearing from Benjamin after Saturday night, then the police would keep up their search for the fugitive.

Perhaps all the way to Southern California

He stared out the plane's small window. There was nothing to see but the night's blackness. For the first time, he considered the consequences if the authorities discovered he and Benjamin had fled together. His son would be taken back to Oregon to face the legal process Patrick Kelly had described. And Micah would be arrested, too: as an accomplice who assisted a suspected felon in his flight across state lines.

His career would be over. And, with it, the possibility that the high school would ever be built.

All of this was in the hands of a group of homeless teenagers.

So be it, he told himself.

I had to do what I've done.

THIRTY-NINE.

It was past midnight when the plane landed. Benjamin wordlessly followed his father through the high-ceilinged terminal and outside to the shuttle bus stop. Even on the empty bus, they sat in different rows and didn't acknowledge one another. It wasn't until they got off and were walking, one behind the other, through the sea of parked vehicles that Micah turned back to his son and spoke.

"So far, so good."

When they reached the BMW, Benjamin stopped and stared.

"This is the same car you had when I ran away."

With the same windshield, Micah thought, that you taped your note on.

A half hour later, the BMW left the freeway behind, gliding down an offramp and heading in the direction of the house. Passing through his old neighborhood, Benjamin grew animated.

"There's the market where Mom and I used to go shopping on Friday afternoons. And there's the park where I hung out with my friends."

There's the convenience store where you set the dumpster on fire, Micah told himself. And next to it is the house that almost burnt down when the fire jumped across the alley.

Micah led the way from the garage to the modest porch. Benjamin followed him inside. He went immediately to his bedroom's open doorway.

The Aerosmith posters on the walls. The desk where he used to complete his homework. The CD player and speakers on top of the chest of drawers. Everything looked the same as the morning he ran away. The teenager stepped forward and slid open the closet door. Inside were his clothes and shoes, untouched since he disappeared.

Micah was sitting at the kitchen table. "It's been a long day," he said. "I'm beat. But we need to talk.

"It's risky for you to stay here. Sooner or later, the neighbors will see you. And there's the chance the cops will come here once they realize I was in Oregon. So tomorrow I'm taking you someplace else to live for a while."

157

*　　*　　*

The next morning, Micah was in the kitchen, dressed in a workout suit and scrambling a skillet full of eggs, when Benjamin appeared. The teenager wolfed down his breakfast. Then he tried on several pieces of clothing from the closet in his room. The pants were too short and the shirts would no longer fit over his shoulders. Micah handed him several of his own blue jeans, but the waists were too wide.

"It looks like you'll have to keep wearing the same clothes for a while," he told Benjamin.

Micah returned to the master bedroom, slipped into a white dress shirt and pulled on a pair of gray slacks. In his bare feet, he went to one of the house's large front windows. There was no one in sight; it was past nine, and the neighbors had left for work.

He pulled on his socks and shoes, grabbed a navy blue blazer and walked with Benjamin to the garage and the BMW.

On the way to the freeway onramp, Micah stopped at a drug store and bought a toothbrush, tooth paste, deodorant and a small bottle of mouthwash. The cashier put the items in a plastic sack. When he returned to the car and handed the sack to his son, Benjamin looked through the contents.

"I haven't used any of these for a while."

"I know."

The teenager stared at his father, a quizzical expression on his face.

As Micah turned the BMW onto the freeway, he saw, out of the corner of his eye, that Benjamin was watching him.

"Did you sleep okay last night?" he asked.

"Not really. I was thinking about a lot of things."

"What kinds of things?"

"If the school district found out you're helping me, do you think they'd fire you?"

Micah kept looking ahead. "They're not going to find out."

"When I lived at home," Benjamin said, "it seemed like you were always at your office. When I woke up, you were already gone—and you were still gone when I went to bed."

The remorse Micah felt so often during the past four years began to creep over him again.

"How come your job means so much to you?" Benjamin said.

Micah shifted in the seat. "Most people work for one reason—to bring a paycheck home. I couldn't stand the thought of living for such a low purpose. When I graduated from college, I wanted to have a career that gave me the chance to do something significant.

"But I hated my first job. I was a paper-pusher at a city planning department, rubber-stamping other people's plans. I began to be afraid that I'd never have the chance to do something really worthwhile with my life.

"Then I found out about a position as a school facility planner. When I got that job, I realized this was the work I was meant to do. There couldn't be a more meaningful career than building new schools.

"Instead of feeling desperate, I felt alive. I had a worthy purpose—in fact, the highest purpose my life could ever have."

He looked at his son.

"In the meantime, I lost you.

"But now I have you back."

*   *   *

Once they reached the city, Micah took the offramp he always used to get to his office. Instead of steering the BMW towards the city's center and the school district headquarters, though, he went south on a major boulevard that ran through the middle of a barrio.

Various shops, restaurants and motels lined both sides of the wide street. Micah picked one of the motels and turned into its driveway. The office was at the front of the long two story building. He told the short, middle-aged Latino at the registration counter that he needed a room for two nights. When the clerk set a clipboard in front of him with a registration form on it, Micah pushed it aside. He paid cash and took the key.

The room was on the second floor at the building's rear. It felt cramped, even though there were almost no furnishings; only a twin bed and a scratched chest of drawers with a small TV set and phone on its surface.

"No one will bother you here," Micah said. He handed Benjamin the room key and a twenty dollar bill. "Try and stay inside. If you get hungry, walk to one of the fast food places we drove past. But bring your meal back here. And don't use the phone. I'll come back after work."

"How long'll I be here?"

Micah didn't know the answer to his question. "Let's talk about that tonight," he said.

FORTY.

His staff members looked up from their work when Micah pushed open the glass door and strode across the bullpen. As he sat behind his desk and surveyed its clutter, Keona came in and took the chair before him.

"I thought you were going to be gone all week."

He'd told her very little about the trip. "I took care of my business faster than I expected. How are things here?"

"Dr. Hernandez calls every morning, asking if I've heard from you.

"There's another call I knew you'd want to hear about," Keona continued. She handed him a message slip with a name and phone number and that morning's date.

"Les Conrad," he read. "Who is he?"

"A detective from the city police department. He sounded anxious to talk with you."

"Did he say why he was calling?"

She shook her head.

The superintendent was at his desk, speaking into the phone in Spanish, when Micah appeared in the open doorway. Dr. Hernandez motioned for him to sit at the conference table.

Across from him on the table's surface was that morning's edition of the newspaper, opened to the opinion page. Near the top of one column was a photo of a woman. Even though it was upside down, she looked familiar. While the old man continued his conversation, Micah pulled the newspaper to his side of the table and turned it towards him.

The woman in the photo was Violet Yeoman. The caption identified her as "School Board Member/Guest Columnist". Above the photo was a headline:

Stop the Unholy School

"Our city is filled with illegal immigrants," the column began. "Because of them, wages are lower, our hospital's emergency room is overwhelmed, poverty and crime stalk our neighborhoods and our schools are overcrowded with the children of non-citizens.

"How has all this happened? It is due to our sins.

"Millions of babies across the U.S.A. have been murdered through abortions. These missing children would have grown up to be productive members of our society. But since they are no longer with us, we see illegal immigrants taking their jobs.

"Many years ago, we expelled God from our schools. Now they are filled with illiterate Spanish speakers, and we are forced to bring scientists and engineers here from India so that our businesses can continue to be competitive.

"Two members of our School Board want to build a new high school at Fairview Plaza. And why is this school needed? Because of our sins, and the illegal immigrants that have come as a result of the sins. This unholy school will encourage more illegal immigration. In the meantime, its presence will destroy the neighborhoods of our fellow citizens and clog the roadways with traffic.

"What is the real solution to the overcrowding at our high schools? It is not spending millions of taxpayer dollars to construct a monstrosity that will ruin the shopping center and change the residents' lives for the worse.

"The solution is this: end abortions, and bring God back into our schools."

When Dr. Hernandez finished his call, he turned to Micah and the newspaper.

"That's a first-class piece of literature, isn't it?" he said. "Because of the State's letter, she feels emboldened. She told me it was time a Board member showed some courage."

The old man watched him. "But we have an even bigger problem. The homeowners behind Raymond Avenue Elementary know about the parking lot. The fact that we'll be encouraging teenagers from all over the city to drive into their neighborhood has got them livid."

Micah leaned forward. "We need to give Myron and Phil some breathing room."

"And how can we do that?" Dr. Hernandez asked impatiently.

"At each Board meeting, the naysayers have been vastly outnumbered. If we hold a community meeting in a large venue like the Madison auditorium, the level of support for the school will be even more striking."

"But you're ignoring some important facts," the superintendent said. "We haven't had a Board meeting since the State sent its letter. We can't be sure of what the public thinks now. And how about the neighbors behind the elementary school? Do you think they're going to be rooting us on?"

The old man shook his head in frustration.

"Goddamn it—you're asking me and the Board members who support the project to roll the dice and hope everything turns out all right. That's not the way a school district should conduct its business."

"The community meeting may be the only way to save the school," Micah said. "Isn't that something worth sticking our necks out for?"

Dr. Hernandez placed his hands together as if in prayer and pressed them against his lips.

"Let me think about this."

As Micah stood, the superintendent spoke again.

"How did it go in Oregon?"

"Not well."

"You couldn't find your son?"

Micah nodded.

FORTY-ONE.

When he returned, Keona followed him into his office.

"Mr. Conrad called again."

After she left him, Micah stared at the phone. The only thing about Conrad's calls that surprised him was how quickly after the flight back from Portland they had come. At least the police would have no clue to Benjamin's whereabouts at the motel.

He picked up the receiver and dialed the detective's number.

"Mr. Wada, thanks for getting back to me." Conrad spoke in a slow, professional manner. "Do you know why I called?"

"No."

"Did you know Connie Carr?"

"Of course. She was a Board member here at the school district."

"She was suffering from health issues that probably led to her death—issues that no doctor had been able to diagnose while she was alive.

"Even though we don't know the cause of death, we suspect her husband had something to do with it."

Micah raised his head.

"Do you know Richard Carr?" Conrad asked.

"I don't."

"We need your help to connect the dots in this case. Richard has been married four times. After Connie's death became public, one of his ex-wives came forward. While they were still together, she discovered he was poisoning her. Every morning, he slipped cyanide into the sugar bowl she used to flavor her coffee.

"Poisoning is the last thing the doctors who treated Connie would be looking for. That's probably why no one could find out what was wrong with her."

Micah's eyes began to fill with tears.

"To move forward," Conrad continued, "we need to find a motive that explains why Richard would want to kill her. A few months back, someone distributed a flyer around the community. It claimed Connie was having affairs with administrators at the district. Did you happen to see it?"

"Yes. Someone left it on my windshield."

"Mr. Wada, how well did you know Connie?"

"Not well."

"Were you and she intimate?" Conrad said.

"No."

For a moment, there was silence on the line.

"I think Richard killed his wife," the detective said. "But without a motive, we can't go after him. You have my number. Please give me a call if you remember anything that might help."

After he replaced the phone in its cradle, Micah wiped at his eyes with the backs of his hands. It wasn't right to conceal the affair with Connie. As the detective told him, this was the information that could bring Richard Carr to justice.

But Micah feared that cooperating with the local police might somehow bring scrutiny of his trip to Oregon—and lead to the discovery of Benjamin's presence.

He picked up the phone again and called Judy.

"When did you get back?" she said.

"Last night."

"Did you see Benjamin?"

Micah hesitated. He wanted her to know the boy was safe. But it made no sense to tell her what had happened.

"I couldn't find him."

"I'm sorry, Micah."

"Is the city still planning to sue the district?" he said.

"I need to close the door. Hold on a second."

He could hear the door creak as she swung it shut. Then she was back on the line.

"At the Council's closed session last night, Don told them a lawsuit will tear the community apart and sour the relationship between the city and the district for years to come."

He's been listening to you after all, Micah thought.

"The council members still think the school shouldn't be built," she said. "They've heard over and over again from Betty and the residents about the traffic and the Latino teenagers. Yet they know Don's right.

"The lawsuit is a line they've drawn in the sand. They're worried that backing away from it now will look like a retreat—or, worse still, a defeat. They've boxed themselves into a corner, and need a way out."

As he listened to Judy, Micah stared at the desk's chaos and confusion. He suddenly realized there was a large brown envelope laying on top of the mess that hadn't been there earlier. Printed on its corner was the State Disbursement Board's Sacramento address.

"Judy, I have to go. I'll call you later."

She was slow to reply.

"All right." She didn't sound pleased.

While he grasped the envelope, Keona came to the office's doorway. "The UPS driver dropped that off right after you left to see the superintendent."

He ripped it open. Inside was a multi-page document on the Disbursement Board's letterhead, addressed to Micah.

"The purpose of this correspondence," it began, "is to clarify the position of the State of California as it relates to a proposed high school at the Fairview Plaza commercial center."

The letter said there had been questions about the suitability of the property and the price the district planned to pay for it. "We have carefully reviewed all of the pertinent documentation, since it is the State's responsibility to insure the district acted in an appropriate manner to protect the health and safety of the school's future students and staff as well as the interests of the taxpayers."

The correspondence recited the findings of the environmental expert who determined the fuel plume was not a danger to those on the site. It pointed out the extraordinary caution the district used by retaining three appraisers to establish the property's value.

"In every respect, the district and its representatives have acted responsibly and within the letter of the law", concluded the letter. "Good luck as you move forward with this much-needed school construction project."

Signed by Sute, it included all of the same cc's as Fred Foster's letter. In addition, it had been copied to the governor's chief of staff.

Micah reached for the phone and dialed Sute's number.

"Have you read my letter?"

"Those are the most beautiful words I've ever set my eyes on," Micah said.

The big man chuckled. "You should've seen Foster's face when I showed it to him. The motherfucker got so excited, I thought he was going to have a stroke. 'The governor's office will never let you send that,' he shouted. 'Well, Fred, I hate to tell you this,' I said. 'But the governor's chief of staff is the one who told me to write it.'"

Sute paused. "How did you get to the governor, anyway?"

"His biggest donor has three young kids who'll go to the school if we ever build it."

Sute guffawed again. "Brilliant! My boss is overjoyed. In Lee's wildest dreams, he never imagined the governor would be the one who discredited Foster and his bullshit."

"We still have some tough issues to work through," Micah cautioned. "For one thing, more residents than ever are angry because of the parking lot on the elementary school playfield."

"I've told you all along—the Disbursement Board's ready to approve the project."

"But the School Board has to approve it first," Micah reminded him. "Will you be in your office this week? I have an idea or two I'd like to run by you."

"I'll be around."

"By the way," Micah said, "did you send the cc's of your letter by UPS?"

"No. Just the original. It'll be a day or so before everyone else gets their copy."

When the call ended, Micah glanced at his watch. It was already one-thirty, and there was much to be done. He picked up the phone again and called Ellen.

"I need to meet with you ASAP."

"What's up?" she said.

"We're going to make some changes to the project."

"Oh? What kinds of changes?"

"Big changes. Can you come by this afternoon?"

"I have a meeting at two-thirty...but I can cancel it."

"Good. I'll see you soon."

Micah kept the phone in his hand as he dialed Kent Hamish's number.

"Are you free at five?" he said to the reporter.

"I'll make myself free. What's going on?"

"Something you'll be very interested in."

He walked into the bullpen and stopped before one of the department's facility planners, a young woman whose assignments included the remodel of Madison Intermediate's auditorium.

"I need Madison's construction drawings."

"You mean the plans for the auditorium remodel?" she said.

"No. The plans for the entire campus. Leave them in the conference room."

Micah made several photocopies of Sute's letter and walked to Dr. Hernandez's office. The door was closed.

"He's with Mr. Richland," the superintendent's secretary, an attractive middle-aged woman, told him from her desk.

"I have to talk with them."

She stared at him. "He doesn't like it when I interrupt his meetings with the Board president."

"He won't mind this time," he said.

She raised her eyebrows and continued to watch him for a moment. Standing, she stepped past him and opened the door. He looked over her shoulder into the room. Dr. Hernandez and Richland were sitting across from one another at the conference table.

"Mr. Wada wants to speak with both of you."

Dr. Hernandez glanced at Richland, who nodded.

The superintendent looked past her to Micah.

"Come in."

He sat next to his boss.

"Myron and I were kicking around the community meeting idea," the old man explained.

"It's the smart thing to do," Richland said. "All along, we've been promising the community members we'd listen to them. This is a good time to show we meant what we said."

"Myron, when should the meeting take place?" Dr. Hernandez said.

"Next week."

"I'll call the rest of the Board members this afternoon."

He turned to Micah. "Do you have anything else for us?"

The assistant superintendent handed each of them a copy of Sute's letter. When the men finished reading it, they glanced at one another. Then Richland looked at Micah.

"How did you get them to write this?"

"The facts are on our side. It was just a matter of time before the State admitted it."

The Board president continued to watch him. "The Sacramento crowd usually doesn't behave so logically."

"This is great news," Dr. Hernandez noted cheerfully.

"I have something else to tell you," Micah said. "Sam Comstock's agreed to accept two million dollars less for the school site."

Richland leaned forward.

"Comstock won't get a dime unless the Board approves the project," Micah said. "If the voters understand the land is a bargain, it'll be easier for you and the rest of the Board to do the right thing."

"I have a feeling this wasn't Comstock's idea," Richland said.

Dr. Hernandez was smiling. "We'll certainly have a few things to brag about at the community meeting."

It was then that Richland startled both of them.

"Hold on a minute!" he shouted, a sullen scowl contorting his features. "This isn't the time for you two to be patting yourselves on the back. My phone's been ringing off the hook. The voters can't believe we're brainless enough to plop the school's parking lot smack in the middle of their neighborhood.

"Unless you come up with a much better way to deal with the parking, I don't think even half of the Board will support the project."

Micah silently met Richland's stare. He stood, turned his back on the pair and walked out of the room.

When he returned to his office, Ellen hadn't arrived. He dialed Denise's number.

"So, you're back."

"I flew into LAX early this morning. Guess what happened when I got to work?"

"Tell me," she said.

"A very important letter was delivered to my office."

"From Sacramento?"

"How did you guess?"

"Call it a woman's intuition. What's it say?"

"That the State was mistaken about the high school." He paused. "Thanks to you, the project is still alive."

"This is going to cost you a lot of dinners."

As Micah listened, he could see her impish grin.

"Well, I always pay my debts. In full."

Across the bullpen, Ellen was pushing open the glass door.

"Speaking of dinner, are you free this Saturday?"

"I think so. I need to check with my babysitter. I'll call you back this afternoon."

Micah emerged from the office and embraced the architect.

"This is all very mysterious!" she whispered. "What are these big changes?"

"Let's go to the conference room."

The facility planner had left the Madison drawings on top of the tables.

"I don't think you've ever visited this school," Micah said, flipping through the oversized pages. He stopped at the site plan.

The auditorium was the centerpiece of the campus. Offices, classroom buildings, the library and cafeteria clustered about it. Behind these were the playfields and portable classrooms. At the rear of the auditorium was a gymnasium and a huge parking lot.

Ellen pushed her long black hair over her shoulders as she studied the plan.

"I haven't been there," she agreed after a moment, glancing up at him. "You say this is an intermediate school?"

He nodded.

"With the large auditorium and parking lot, it looks more like a high school."

"That's what it used to be."

"Why are you showing me this?" Ellen asked.

"You said Fairview Plaza would make a decent school site if students didn't drive to it."

She tilted her head, a questioning look on her face.

"What are you getting at?"

"If we used the land saver money to build an intermediate school at the Plaza, the traffic issues would be solved. Seventh and eighth graders are too young to drive."

"But that doesn't relieve the high school overcrowding."

"Are you sure?"

Ellen's eyes suddenly widened. "It does," she said, "if you move the Madison students to the land saver school—"

"And use Madison as a high school." He placed his open palm on the drawing.

"What's Madison's enrollment?"

"Just over eleven hundred."

"And the land saver project is designed for twelve hundred," the architect said. "Perfect!"

"Let's go visit Madison," he said.

They drove slowly past the auditorium and the other buildings at the front of the site, turned onto the street that bordered the playfields and portable classrooms and circled around to the rear of the school.

He pulled into the parking lot and stopped near the gym's entrance. Classes were over for the day and the campus was almost empty. Several boys were leaving the building. They wore t-shirts and shorts, and one bounced a basketball as he walked.

Micah and Ellen walked past the teenagers and went inside. Grandstands towered over either side of the basketball court. Beyond the court were boys and girls locker rooms and a doorway which led outside to the rear of the adjacent auditorium.

The pair entered the auditorium through an unlocked side door. Standing beside the stage, they stared at the sea of fixed theatre seats.

"There must be room here for a thousand spectators," Ellen said.

They stepped up the auditorium's center aisle and moved on, visiting every one of the campus' remaining buildings.

When they returned to the BMW and slipped inside, the architect turned to Micah.

"It wouldn't take much work or money to get this facility ready for high school students," she said.

"You're right. There's something I have to find out, though."

He glanced around them at the simple, aging houses that surrounded the school.

"The teenagers and traffic would be coming here, instead of to the Plaza. I need to know what our neighbors will think about Madison becoming a high school again.

"The Board members and Dr. Hernandez will string me up if I resolve one crisis by starting a brand new one."

FORTY-TWO.

Hamish was sitting outside Micah's office when he returned. Now it was the assistant superintendent who had a game-changing letter from the State to share.

"They've switched their positions," the reporter said after he read Sute's correspondence. "What happened?"

"You'll have to ask them."

"Oh, I will. What does this letter mean for the district?"

"That we have a real chance to end this obscene over-crowding." If our Board lets us, Micah added to himself.

After Hamish left, he glanced at his watch. It was almost six. He shut out the lights and locked the glass entry door behind him.

For a moment, he stared across the parking lot. He was anxious to drive to the motel. But he needed to talk to Chimalma. And her banged-up Fiesta was parked beside his shiny BMW.

The parent coordinators' so-called office consisted of nothing more than a single metal desk and several filing cabinets, squeezed into an alcove at the end of a hallway.

Halfway down the hallway, Micah stopped. There was no light in the alcove. He was about to turn on his heels and return to the parking lot when he heard Chimalma's voice, speaking Span-ish. He carefully took several steps forward. A scribbling sound told him that, despite the darkness, she was writing in her notebook.

After a moment, he heard her replace the phone on its cradle. She switched the desk light on.

"You're here very late," she said.

"So are you."

The young woman shrugged. "At the end of the day, there's always something left to do."

"I need to talk with you."

Chimalma kept her dark eyes on him as he sat down.

"We're going to build an intermediate school at Fairview Plaza," he said. "That will end the neighbors' concerns about traffic and parking."

"You mean there wouldn't be a new high school?"

For the first time, Micah heard anger in her voice.

"The overcrowding can't go on any longer," she insisted impatiently.

He raised his open palms in front of his chest, as though trying to hold back her displeasure.

"We'll have another high school—on the Madison campus."

The tension that had crossed her face began to soften. "Where would the Madison students go?"

"To the land saver project."

"The high school at Madison—will it still be a fundamental school?"

"Probably. Dr. Hernandez thinks it's best for the students. And the public likes the idea."

"How many students can Madison hold?" she said.

"Twelve hundred."

"So each of the two existing high schools would only lose six hundred students?"

"That depends on how many kids who would've attended private high schools go to Madison instead."

She focused a steely stare on him.

"If our project is picked to be the land saver school, you'll be saving millions of dollars. You must use that money to end the overcrowding once and for all. You must build more classrooms at Madison."

The old campus' conversion would likely be the final opportunity to end the district's facility crisis. As Chimalma was saying, this opportunity must not be wasted. He hadn't thought of expanding Madison. But she was absolutely right.

Chimalma stared at him a moment longer.

"Every night before I fall asleep, I study my Bible," she said. "Last evening, I read the story of your namesake, the prophet Micah. I learned that he rebelled against the social wrongs of his time. That he was a protector of the poor and powerless." She looked into his eyes. "Now I'm more sure than ever that you will do the right thing."

Without another word, she turned back to her notepad.

While the sound of Micah's footsteps echoed down the hallway of the empty building, Chimalma set the notepad aside and switched off the desk lamp. She pulled her purse out from under the desk and removed her wallet. Inside was a picture of her son, standing in front of the Catholic church where he had been baptized.

In the darkness, Chimalma's eyes filled with tears that rolled down her plump brown cheeks.

"Usted va a tener lo que se merece," she said aloud, her low voice cracking with emotion.

You are going to have what you deserve.

FORTY-THREE.

Micah drove through the twilight to the motel. When he walked up the stairs and knocked on the door, there was no response. He knocked again, more loudly this time, but still his son didn't answer. Now Micah wished he had gotten two room keys. He considered going to the office and asking for another, but decided instead to return to the BMW and wait.

Fifteen minutes later, he saw Benjamin. The teenager was walking casually past the office and along the side of the building. He held a white paper sack from Kentucky Fried Chicken. By the time Micah got out of the car, Benjamin had already begun to climb the stairs to the second floor. He didn't realize his father was following him until he stopped at the door and saw Micah out of the corner of his eye as he fished in his pocket for the key.

"Hey," he said.

"Hey yourself."

There were no chairs, so they sat next to each other on the end of the bed. Benjamin rested the sack between them and tore it open, exposing a collection of chicken parts and several paper napkins.

"Want some?"

"Sure." He grasped a leg with his fingers.

While Benjamin picked up a wing, Micah asked: "How was your day?"

He shrugged. "Pretty boring, actually. How long'll I have to stay here?" He sounded forlorn.

"I don't know yet."

"What'll happen after you find someplace for me to live?"

"We'll create a new identity for you."

"A new identity?" Benjamin repeated, gaping at his father.

"You'll need a new name, with the documentation to prove it's yours. That will allow you to live a normal life, to get an education and have a job."

Micah paused. "It'll allow you to get married some day and raise a family. With a different identity, you'll have a future."

"How will we get these documents?"

"I have to find that out."

It was then that Micah noticed Benjamin's clothes.

"Did you get a new shirt and blue jeans?"

Benjamin nodded. "At a store up the street."

"All I gave you this morning was twenty dollars. Cash must go a long way in this neighborhood."

"I had some money left after I bought my airline ticket," Benjamin said without looking his father in the eyes.

Micah set the leg bone back in the torn paper sack.

"If you're arrested," he said, wiping his fingers on a napkin, "the first thing the police will do is take your fingerprints. They'll transmit them to Washington, D.C., where the FBI maintains a database with prints from crime scenes all across the U.S.

"In a day or so, the police will know they have Welund in their cell. And then you and I will probably go to prison for a long time."

"You don't have to worry about that," Benjamin replied indignantly. "I didn't steal these clothes."

He wasn't telling the truth. Indeed, he had gotten the shirt and jeans at a store up the street. But he hadn't purchased them. The teenager was immature enough to believe there was very little risk to him—or anyone else—in tucking them under his arm and marching out while the store's lone clerk helped another customer. After all, he needed new clothes, and stealing was the way he got what he needed or wanted.

Besides, he was bored. And there was nothing better for breaking up a boring afternoon than a little shoplifting.

"For the rest of your life," Micah said, "you'll have to avoid being arrested. We can change your identity. But there's no way to change your fingerprints."

In silence, they finished eating the chicken. Benjamin scooped up the sack full of bones, went into the bathroom and stuffed it into a tiny plastic trash can. He re-joined his father on the end of the bed, reached out to the TV and switched it on. That night's Angels baseball game appeared on the screen.

"Remember when the three of us used to go to Anaheim Stadium?" Micah said.

Benjamin nodded. "I'd look forward to it all week."

His mother attended college on a softball scholarship and was an enthusiastic and knowledgeable baseball fan. Each spring morning after Micah left for work, she would begin a daily ritual while her little boy sat next to her. Spreading the day's sports section on the kitchen table, she reviewed the highlights of the previous evening's game. Next, she described the pitcher who was starting that night.

"Mike Witt has a great fastball. I just wish he threw his curve more often," she'd say in her girlish voice, her sky blue eyes focused on him.

After they finished with the sports section and had breakfast, they walked outside to the family's Ford station wagon. His elementary school was only a mile from the house. But she liked to drop him off on her way to work. With a gentle smile, she watched him as he climbed out of the Ford and made his way across the lawn to the front entrance.

She picked him up after school and took him with her as she completed various errands. Every night, she helped him with his homework. Her sensitivity and patience almost made up for Micah's absences, which only grew more frequent as his responsibilities at the district increased. He stopped taking Benjamin to the library, and the three of them no longer went to Angels games together. But she never let her son feel alone or neglected.

And then, like the most frightening and unexpected nightmare imaginable, the cancer came.

Micah and Benjamin watched the game for several innings. They rarely spoke except to comment on a particular play or batter.

Finally, Micah stood.

"I'd better get home. I'll come by tomorrow at lunch time."

Benjamin wrapped his arms around his father. As the pair held each other, Micah whispered into his son's ear.

"Watch out for yourself."

"You, too."

Once he was sitting behind the BMW's steering wheel in the parking lot's gloom, Micah paused. He wondered if he should go back up the stairs and spend the night with Benjamin. The teenager seemed lonely and depressed. But he didn't have a change of clothes with him or a way to shave when he awoke.

After a few minutes, he started the engine and drove to the freeway onramp.

Benjamin was standing on the second floor landing, watching the car. When its headlights came on and it pulled out of the lot, he went to the motel's office, asked the clerk for a pen and returned to the room. He pulled a napkin out of the trash can and set it on top of the chest of drawers. While the Angels game droned on beside him, he leaned forward and methodically printed out a message in large, simple letters.

When he finished, he placed the pen on top of the note. He tossed the key onto the bed, walked out of the room and disappeared into the night.

FORTY-FOUR.

On the way to his office the next morning, Micah stopped at the 7-11 store. Copies of that morning's newspaper were stacked next to the register.

At the top of the front page, in bold capital letters, was this headline:

STATE: SCHOOL SITE IS SAFE

Micah picked up several copies. Back in the parked car, he began to read the story. As he did so, a self-satisfied smile crept across his face. Hamish had asked the school's most prominent opponents to comment on Sute's letter—a document they didn't know existed and had not read. They sounded flustered and unsure of themselves.

"This doesn't seem possible," Betty Phelan said of the new letter. She had talked with Fred Foster many times over the last several months. During each of their conversations, he assured her the land saver project was as good as dead and buried.

She was furious that the State, for whatever inexplicable reason, had sent this second letter. But what made her even angrier was Foster's failure to pick up the phone and warn her it was coming. As she tried to answer Hamish's questions, the councilwoman knew she sounded like a fool.

"Are you still opposed to the high school?" the reporter said.

"Of course!"

"Why?"

"Because—"

Phelan stopped. She had almost revealed the real reason for her opposition: that her constituents believed the new school would draw gangbangers into their neighborhood.

The councilwoman was considering a run for the State Senate. That meant appealing for much broader political support then had been required to win her Council seat. It was one thing to cater to the fears of her affluent neighbors. It was quite another to seek votes from those who lived outside the city limits. Many of those voters were Latinos.

"Because of the traffic!" she snapped.

"If the district solves the traffic issues, will you drop your opposition?"

By this point in the interview, Phelan had collected her thoughts. She recalled the Council's closed session earlier in the week, and Don Smith's warning of what would happen if the fight with the school district went on. She couldn't let her opponents in the senate race portray her as an enemy of public education.

"This would be a perfect time for the School Board to show it's interested in working with the rest of us," she said. "Instead of trying to shove the project down everyone's throat."

*　　　*　　　*

Micah was sitting at his desk when Keona arrived for work. He motioned for her to come into his office. After she sat down, he handed her the newspaper.

The secretary stared, wide-eyed, at the headline.

"Wow! Maybe we'll get to build the high school after all."

"You live near Madison, don't you?"

She nodded. "It's six blocks away. My kids went there."

"That's where the high school will be located."

"Not at the Plaza?"

He leaned back in his chair and told Keona about the plan to convert Madison to a high school and use the land saver funding to construct an intermediate school at the shopping center.

"Good idea!" she exclaimed.

"What will your neighbors think about converting Madison?"

"Most of the households have kids. The parents will be overjoyed to hear there's going to be a high school nearby."

"What about the traffic?"

"Except for a few minutes at the beginning and end of the day, there won't be all that many extra cars. Anyway, what's a little inconvenience if it means our sons and daughters are going to have a first-class education?"

She kept her eyes on her boss. "Madison's a much better location than the Plaza. The idea of building a parking lot at Raymond Avenue Elementary…" Her voice trailed off.

"Yeah. That wasn't such a great idea. Why didn't you say something before?"

"Because you were so excited about it. You were sure it'd solve the traffic problems. And Dr. Hernandez agreed with you. But you're right—I should've told you what a dumb idea it was.

"I promise I'll never keep my mouth shut again."

They stared at each other and began to laugh.

Next he called Judy, who agreed to meet him at the Starbucks near the city hall. On the way to the coffee shop, he parked on the street with the rows of apartment buildings. There were For Rent signs before several of them, including the one where the meeting with the Latino parents had taken place. Micah copied the phone numbers onto his ever-present pad of yellow paper.

As he stood there, people kept passing him by. Vendors pushing carts full of vegetables. Mothers and grandmothers leading small children or pushing strollers. Workers who were here to make repairs or clean carpets, unloading supplies and equipment from the beds of pick-up trucks and the backs of vans.

Except for Micah, everyone on the sidewalk was Latino. He realized Benjamin would stand out like a sore thumb. Sooner or later, the police who patrolled the neighborhood would notice his presence and wonder why a young Anglo was living on this street.

Judy arrived at the coffee shop a few minutes late and sat across from him at a small corner table.

"The Mixer was only a few days ago. But it seems like a lot longer than that since I've seen you," he said.

She didn't answer.

He stood and, a few minutes later, returned with their coffees.

"This morning's front page surprised everyone at city hall," she said. "Don can't figure out how you got the new letter out of the State."

"Yesterday, you told me the Council is boxed in," he said. "I'm going to give them a way out.

"We're converting the Madison campus to a high school and using the land saver funding to build an intermediate school. There'll still be extra traffic around the Plaza. But there won't be any teenage drivers. And there won't be a parking lot on Raymond Avenue's playfield.

"Will this satisfy the Council?"

She stared at him. "I think it will."

"We need a meeting with Phelan, Richland, Don and Dr. Hernandez. A meeting where we can resolve our differences once and for all."

She kept watching him.

"I'll make it happen," she promised.

He reached across the table and took her hand.

"Where do things stand between you and Don?"

She glanced down at their fingers, entwined on the table top. Then she raised her head, looked him in the eyes and pulled her hand away.

"I'm always going to be honest with you," she said. "Remember what I told you at the Mixer? My job means everything to me."

She pushed her chair from the table. "I have to get back to city hall and tell Don the good news," she announced.

They gazed at one another for a moment longer before she walked out of the coffee shop.

After she had gone, he continued to watch the empty doorway. He almost got up and followed her. But he knew this would be pointless. She'd decided what was important to her.

When he finally left the Starbucks, Micah stopped on the sidewalk and stood alone in the late morning sunlight. It was a warm, clear day. Just down the street was the bar he and Judy had visited on the first day they met. He could see the small neon sign, extending over its front door at a perpendicular angle so those who passed could easily read its three words.

Monkey Bar
Cocktails

He remembered the bar's darkened interior.

A shelter from everything and everyone outside.

A sanctuary that held the ingredients for any cocktail he could imagine.

A hideaway where someone could sit alone, undisturbed—

And drink so much liquor that his troubles would be obliterated.

But he needed to visit Benjamin. Needed to tell his son he would be staying at the motel for a few more days.

Once again, there was no answer to Micah's knocks. When he tried the knob, the motel room's door swung open. He noticed the bed's spread and blanket had not been pulled back. Then he saw the room key, laying in the middle of the bed.

The TV was on. Micah turned his head toward the sound. On top of the chest of drawers was one of the paper napkins from the Kentucky Fried Chicken sack. He realized it was filled with Benjamin's large, simple printing.

He didn't pick up the napkin right away. He dreaded what it might say.

Finally, he grasped a corner of the thin, stained tissue, sat on the edge of the bed and read the note.

DAD—
I HAVE PUT YOU IN A BAD SITUATION. YOU ALREADY STUCK YOUR NECK WAY OUT BY GOING TO OREGON AND GETTING ME OUT OF THERE. IF I STAY AROUND, I KNOW YOU WILL KEEP TRYING TO HELP ME. AS LONG AS YOU DO THIS, YOU ARE RISKING EVERYTHING THAT IS IMPORTANT TO YOU. JUST BEING SEEN WITH ME IS ENOUGH FOR YOU TO LOSE YOUR JOB AND GO TO PRISON. I WILL BE ALL RIGHT. SOME DAY, YOU WILL HEAR FROM ME AGAIN. I LOVE YOU.
                                        —YOUR SON

Micah stared at the napkin for several minutes. Breathing heavily, he finally took it in both hands, pressed it against his face and began to sob. His tears soaked its grimy surface until the ink from Benjamin's message smeared his cheeks.

*   *   *

The Grimm Farm site was just a few miles to the south of the motel; it only took Micah five minutes to drive there. Construction workers swarmed about the property. They were finishing the framing of the classroom buildings and installing utility conduit and concrete walkways.

He stopped at the contractor's trailer. The job super-intendent and one of the subcontractors were standing before a makeshift table, hunched over a set of plans, when he stepped inside and wordlessly lifted a yellow hard hat from a rack on the wall next to the door.

The superintendent raised his head. "Mr. Wada. Ned told me you stopped by on Saturday. Here to walk the project? I'll be free in a minute."

While the man turned back to the subcontractor and the plans, Micah went outside. He dodged the busy workers as he walked along the perimeters of the buildings; several times, he stopped to survey the activity around him.

There was a life-and-death reason why he chose to come here. His career was the one thing in his life that made him feel good about himself. Watching the construction of the new school, he felt the deadly despair lifting; his thoughts began to turn away from the deep, dark, suicidal depression.

Soon, he reached the old farmhouse at the far end of the property. The contractor planned to begin remodeling it within a few days. The interior would be reconstructed, following the original hand drawn plans for the rooms that the Grimm sisters had provided to the district. Most of the house's windows were still boarded over. The one exception was a small, square opening at the edge of the building.

Without warning, a face appeared in the opening. It was a Latino in his twenties. While Micah watched, the man stuck his head out the window and into the sunlight, as if he wanted to make sure he was seen. His head was shaved, and an assortment of crudely applied tattoos covered his skull, face and neck.

"What are you doing here?" Micah demanded loudly.

The intruder glared at him.

"Get the fuck off of my school site!"

Behind him, Micah heard footsteps. He looked over his shoulder to see the job superintendent and Terry Rivers.

"We have a trespasser," he announced.

"What do you mean?" Rivers asked his boss.

Micah turned back to the small window.

It was empty.

FORTY-FIVE.

That afternoon, Micah closed the door to his office, picked up the phone and dialed Les Conrad's number.

"I wasn't telling you the truth," he said to the detective. "Connie and I were having an affair."

He described their rendezvous at the hotel and how she was suddenly afflicted with the rashes and lesions that ultimately ended their relationship.

"Why didn't you tell me this before?"

Micah hesitated. "I preferred that no one knew."

"Why did you change your mind?"

"My conscience got to me. I can't let her husband get away with this."

"How did you see the flyer about her alleged affairs?"

Micah told Conrad about the figure lurking outside the apartments who had slipped it under his windshield wiper.

"Can you give me a description of this individual?"

"Not really. It was dark, and he wore a trench coat and a ski cap pulled down over his forehead."

"How do you know it was a man?"

"Because whoever it was happened to be very tall."

"How tall would you say?"

"Well over six feet. By the way, he drove a pick-up truck with a camper shell."

"How do you know that?"

Micah described seeing the truck parked behind his BMW. "I spotted a similar truck once when I was leaving the hotel after meeting Connie."

"Richard Carr is six foot six," said Conrad. "And he owns a pick-up truck with a camper shell."

Micah let out a long breath.

"Were you in love with Connie?" asked the detective.

"I wouldn't say that."

"So your relationship was all about sex?"

"We had more than that."

"Was she in love with you?"

Micah didn't answer immediately. "I don't know."

There was silence for a moment.

"Thanks for getting hold of me," Conrad said. "Now I've got quite a few things to do."

The following afternoon, he called Micah.

"We obtained a search warrant and surprised Carr this morning at his house. He kept a diary of Connie's activities, including her liaisons with other men. It records the dates and times when he saw you and her enter and leave the hotel.

"So now we have the motive we need."

"Where's Richard?" Micah said.

"In the county jail—where he'll stay until the trial begins."

FORTY-SIX.

That evening, Micah was about to get up from his desk and drive home when the phone rang.

"Mr. Wada," said an older man's gruff voice, "Sullivan Desmond here. I'm a producer at CNN's headquarters in Atlanta.

"We're looking into an unusual murder case. Our sources tell us a board member at the San Juan Cajon School District died recently under suspicious circumstances. Her husband is suspected of poisoning her."

"Why are you calling me?" Micah said.

"Because we understand you're a material witness—that you can testify to the husband's motive. Is the information I have about your role in the case accurate?"

The ordeal he had been through to try and obtain the land saver funding taught Micah a hard lesson: The way facts are presented to the public can be just as important as the facts themselves. After all, the opponents' twisting of the facts had nearly ended the opportunity to build the new school.

With Benjamin out of the picture, Micah wanted nothing more than to take Richard Carr down for what he had done to Connie. An interview with CNN presented a golden opportunity to put Carr on trial in the court of public opinion. On prime time, he'd describe her body, covered with wounds, and the pain and suffering he watched her endure. He'd tell the host that her poisoning was death by torture. Micah's emotionally loaded comments would make it more likely than ever that Carr was not only convicted, but received the most severe penalty possible from the judge and jury.

"Mr. Wada, are you still there?"

"I'm here."

"Are you the material witness?"

"Yes, I am."

"We'd like to send someone from our Atlanta office to interview you for a segment on our national broadcast."

"That's fine," Micah said. "But I don't want anyone to know about this until the interview has taken place."

"That's the way we'd like to handle it, too," Desmond said. "I'll get back to you tomorrow morning to work out the details."

FORTY-SEVEN.

On the evening of the community meeting, Ellen and her assistant arrived at the Madison auditorium an hour early. The campus lot was already full; they had to park several blocks away. The two women squeezed their way past a group of Latino parents who were standing at the auditorium's side doorway, trying to enter.

All of the seats were occupied. Those just arriving had to stand in the aisles or the building's lobby. The sound of the audience members rumbled through the structure's vaulted ceiling. Many held large placards with handwritten messages in both English and Spanish, urging the Board to build the new high school.

A long table had been positioned in the center of the stage with folding chairs behind it. At the side of the table was a podium and a microphone stand. A large white screen stood against the stage's rear wall, behind the chairs; in front of the screen, an overhead projector had been placed on a gray metal stand.

Several of those who were to sit at the table began to mount the stage. Soon, Dr. Hernandez, Myron Richland and Phil Putnam were in their chairs. Violet Yeoman and Jon Laird had also been invited to attend the meeting, but both refused to participate. Two vacant chairs marked their absence.

Ellen and her assistant briefly tested the overhead projector before joining Micah in the auditorium's first row of seats.

A few minutes after 7 p.m., Richland got to his feet and strode to the podium. The huge crowd became quiet.

"Thanks for coming out tonight," the Board president began. "The school district called this meeting to report on the status of the new high school and hear your comments. But first, I want to share some brand new information about the project.

"The residents near Fairview Plaza are concerned about the traffic the high school will create. And the Board wants this project to work for everyone."

He hesitated, surveying the audience. "To achieve that goal, we plan to build an intermediate school at the Plaza and establish the fundamental high school here on the Madison campus."

A murmur moved through the crowd as those in the auditorium tried to understand what Richland had just told them.

Suddenly, a young man near the front of the audience stood. It was Danny Aguilar.

"Are we getting a high school or not?" he shouted impatiently.

This caused many others to raise their own voices.

Richland lifted his hands high above his head.

"Hold on. Let me explain again what's going to happen."

The hubbub began to subside.

"We're building a new intermediate school at the Plaza," he repeated, "and moving the Madison students there. Then we're converting the Madison site into a high school."

The voices rose again.

Richland pulled the mic closer to his face. "Our architect is here to show you what we plan to do."

He introduced Ellen and asked her to come forward. While her assistant stood at the projector, changing the overhead slides on the screen, Ellen reviewed the site plans for the new intermediate school and then the improvements which would be made to the Madison campus.

The images of Madison Fundamental High School that flashed on the screen included a rendering of a large new two story classroom wing at the edge of the playfield.

"This additional building will increase the school's capacity by almost a thousand students," Ellen promised.

"It will be enough classrooms to relieve the overcrowding at both the existing high schools."

At the end of her presentation, the architect stepped down from the stage and returned to her seat next to Micah.

For a moment, the massive room was eerily silent.

Someone in the crowd clapped his hands together.

Another pair of hands began clapping at the back of the building.

Here and there throughout the throng, more clapping started.

In no time, the applause rolled across every part of the auditorium.

Soon it was deafening.

Ellen turned in her seat to watch the audience.

There were many Anglos. But the majority were Latinos.

Brown faces beaming, brown hands clapping as they celebrated the coming end to decades of school overcrowding.

She looked at Micah, who had barely said a word to her since she arrived. He was staring towards the stage as if in a world of his own.

She covered his hand with her own.

"You did it, Micah!" she said loudly, trying to make herself heard above the audience.

He turned to her, a blank look on his face. Then the light came back into his eyes. A broad smile began to cross his features. He put his arm around Ellen's slim shoulders and pulled her to him.

"It's amazing what a little magic can accomplish, isn't it?" he whispered into her ear.

FORTY-EIGHT.

The driver was steering the flatbed truck through a curve when he spotted Benjamin up ahead. The teenager stood alone, thumb extended, in the sweltering late summer heat.

"Where you headed?" the driver asked.

"Search me. What about you?"

"North to pick up a load of redwood."

They didn't say more than a few words to one another until, an hour later, the truck slowed as it entered a little town.

"I'll get out here," Benjamin said. This looks as good as any place else, he told himself.

Walking along the vacant sidewalk, past several boarded-up storefronts, he came to a diner and pushed its screen door open. All seven tables were unoccupied. A spindly old bald man in a stained T-shirt stood behind the counter.

The stranger sat on a stool before him.

"Is it always so quiet?" he said.

"Oh, folks'll start comin in round dinnertime. What can I get you?"

"A hamburger and Coke."

"You want cheese on that?"

"No."

"Onions?"

"Nope."

The old man turned.

"Sergio," he said to a Latino whose sad face was visible through a wide opening in the wall.

"I heard him, Earl."

The cook slid the patty onto the hot grill, sending up a sharp hissing that filled the empty room.

"I'm looking for a job," Benjamin said.

Earl placed his large hands on the counter top.

"I haven't got anything right now. But they're usually hirin at the packin shed this time of year. It's the start of the pickin season."

"What's being picked?"

"Pears, of course. This county's the pear capital of America," he said proudly.

Sergio handed a plate with the hamburger and a pile of French fries to the old man, who set it in front of the stranger.

Before he bit into the sandwich, Benjamin asked: "Where's the packing shed?"

"A couple of miles up the road. You can't miss it."

The shed was, indeed, hiring. The manager, a stocky man in his mid-thirties named Leonardo, handed him an employment application.

After a few minutes, Benjamin looked up from the paper.

"It says I need a picture ID and Social Security number."

"They're not hard to get." He spoke with the hint of a Spanish accent.

Benjamin cocked his head as he listened to the man.

"Where are you staying?" the manager said.

Benjamin shrugged.

"You can sleep here tonight." Leonardo nodded towards the shed as he spoke. "There's a cot in the back room."

The next morning, another Latino pulled up to the front of the paintless wooden building in a white Dodge panel van. While Benjamin watched, he opened the back doors. The van's interior had been turned into a mobile photo studio.

The man snapped his picture and handed Benjamin an Application For Documents. The first line asked him to provide his name. He hesitated for a moment before printing, in large block letters, MIKE WITT.

The man looked over the completed form.

"That's the name of a baseball player, isn't it? He pitched for the Angels. Threw a no-hitter one season."

"A perfect game," Mike corrected.

The man stared at him. "Right you are. You know your baseball. Tomorrow, I'll bring the documents back. They'll cost a hundred dollars."

"I haven't got that kind of money."

"Leonardo says you're good for it. I'll come by again after you've cashed your first paycheck."

Mike began as a sorter, removing damaged fruit from the packing line. Within a few weeks, he was moved down the line to help pack the pears into forty-five pound boxes. Like most of the jobs at the shed, this was seasonal work that would keep him employed for only another month or so.

By then, though, Leonardo had made the teenager his assistant. He taught Mike how to maintain the numerous pieces of specialized equipment that filled the shed.

With the manager's help, he was also picking up some Spanish. The man began to call him Miguel. Several nights a week, Leonardo would invite him to dinner in the little wood frame house on the edge of an orchard where he lived with his wife and two teenage daughters.

Over a meal of grilled chicken, beans and tortillas, Leonardo shared the story of how, twenty years before, the couple had come to live in this isolated region. Born and raised in the poverty of Oaxaca's highlands, the young lovers heard from one of Leonardo's great uncles of a land north of Napa Valley where there was plenty of work picking fruit. So they trekked two thousand miles to the U.S. border, stayed in Mexicali until they found someone to lead them into California, then traveled another seven hundred miles before arriving at their destination: a countryside of steep hills, jagged volcanic outcroppings and high plateaus.

Within a few days, Leonardo began working at the shed.

One evening after dinner, the men sat on a sofa in the cramped living room, watching a Giants baseball game. Leonardo set his can of Budweiser on the scarred Formica table before them.

"You've got a pretty good job, with a regular paycheck. You saving any money?"

Miguel shook his head.

"You need to think about the future. I'll take you to the bank and show you how to open an account."

Every payday, Miguel followed the rutted dirt road from the shed to the deteriorating, half-empty downtown. On one particular Friday, he parked Leonardo's old Ford pick-up truck before the bank building.

Just as he was about to get out of the truck, a hulking figure emerged from the bank. Wearing a black hoodie that covered his features, the man lumbered across the vacant sidewalk.

Through the open side window, he raised the barrel of a pistol until it was pointed at Miguel's face.

"Let me in!" he demanded.

The teenager leaned across the patched bench seat, pushed down on the handle and nudged the door ajar.

While he continued to point the pistol at Miguel, the robber used his opposite hand, which already grasped a large canvas sack, to awkwardly snag the edge of the door and pull it open. As he tried to slide his bulk onto the seat, he had trouble juggling the pistol and the sack.

Seeing this, Miguel pulled the key from the ignition and pushed open the driver side door. Without looking back, he sprinted across the street and into the diner.

Realizing that Miguel had taken the key with him, the grossly overweight robber climbed back out of the cab and began to trudge along the sidewalk, the pistol in one hand and the sack of bills in the other. At the end of the block, he went around the corner of a brick building and disappeared.

Most of the diner's tables were filled. Miguel walked quickly across the room to the counter.

"You're in a hurry today," Earl said.

He didn't answer.

"The usual?"

The teenager nodded.

As the smell of frying ground beef rose from the grill, the old man stared past Miguel. Then he limped around the counter and between the tables before pausing beside one of the windows facing the street.

"Somethin's goin on over at the bank," he said loudly to no one in particular.

The diners turned their heads. Several bank tellers stood on the opposite sidewalk, talking excitedly with townsfolk who happened to be passing by.

At that moment, a black sheriff's cruiser pulled to the curb behind the pick-up truck.

"Shit!" Miguel muttered.

While everyone else kept their eyes on the scene in front of the bank, he turned towards the kitchen.

Ten minutes later, a sheriff's deputy and a man in his forties who was wearing a business suit marched through the diner's doorway.

"There he is!" The man pointed at Miguel, sitting alone at the counter.

He wanted to stand and rush out of the room. But he knew it was too late for that.

While Miguel stood, the man approached him. A look of gratitude filled his plain, clean-shaven features.

"I'm Jacob Toft, the bank manager," he said as he shook the startled teenager's hand. "Thank you for what you did."

Earl stood beside the pair.

"What's this all about?" he asked.

"A thug robbed the bank this afternoon—and tried to force our friend here to help him make his getaway. But he ran over here with the key to his truck, leaving the culprit with no way to get out of town."

"We picked the robber up a few minutes ago," said the deputy.

"Where'd you find the son-of-a-bitch?" Earl asked, his hands on his hips.

"Around the corner, sitting on the curb. He'd twisted his ankle."

The old man cackled wickedly. "A real master criminal!"

"You're one of our customers, aren't you?" Toft said.

Miguel nodded.

At that moment, a young woman who wore a black dress with white polka dots walked in with a Nikon camera in her hands.

"We'd like to get a picture of you and Mr. Toft," she told Miguel.

He shook his head. "I don't have time. I'm on my lunch break. I've got to get back to work."

The bank manager put his hand on the teenager's shoulder.

"Your boss won't mind. Not after he hears what you've done."

"No," he insisted. "I've got to go."

He took a step towards the door, but the deputy shuffled into his path.

"I'll make everything right with your boss," the cop assured him.

Reluctantly, Miguel followed Toft and the secretary outside and across the street to the front of the bank. He frowned as the banker grasped his hand and grinned at the camera. The woman took numerous shots from various angles. She kept trying to get him to smile, but he ignored her pleas.

When she was finished, Miguel wordlessly turned his back on the pair. He stalked to the pick-up, started the engine and drove away.

"He didn't seem too happy about bein a hero," said Earl, standing on the opposite side of the street next to the deputy. "Or gettin his picture taken."

The deputy glanced at the old man.

"Do you know where he works?"

"Yup. The packin shed."

The deputy rubbed the back of his hand across his chin as he stared up the street at the truck, moving towards the horizon.

EPILOGUE.

June, 2001

Through the open bedroom window, Chimalma could hear the rude, high-pitched caws of the sea gulls. Even though her apartment was ten miles from the ocean, the birds had become a daily presence, picking through the garbage at the dumpster down the alleyway. Their grating calls reminded her of the seaside village where she was born. When she was a girl, they always seemed to be gliding overhead, noisily waiting for her father and the other fishermen to return with their catch.

It wasn't like her to stay in bed after she awoke. There was always something to be done: breakfast to prepare for her son, Julio; and after that, notes to compose and files to update and phone calls to make. She and the other parent coordinators were as busy as ever.

On this morning, though, she was in no hurry to raise her head from the pillow. Instead, she watched the ceiling fan, rotating slowly above her, and thought of the day ahead.

That afternoon, Madison Fundamental High School's first group of seniors would be receiving their diplomas. And Julio, as the valedictorian—the highest achieving student in the entire graduating class—would be among the ceremony's speakers.

A handful of their relatives lived in Southern California and planned to join Chimalma. But at this moment, she was remembering the relations who would not be there. Over the years, she'd written many letters to her parents; they never prompted a response. As for Julio's father, she had no way of knowing how to contact him.

She used to wonder how her life might have turned out if he'd stayed behind with her in the village, or took her with him when the carnival packed up and left. She understood these were nothing more than a teenager's romantic fantasies. Still, that didn't stop her from wishing one or the other had come true—especially after she'd traveled, alone and pregnant, to the U.S. and struggled to make her way in this strange new country.

Before becoming a parent coordinator, she held a series of mundane and often degrading jobs. This included working as a maid at a large luxury hotel adjacent to the world's most famous amusement park. After she cleaned a room, the bell hop would ask her to show it to him. Then, a few minutes later, he'd return with a businessman from out of town and a high-priced hooker. Once the couple finished their lovemaking, Chimalma was expected to return to the room to change the bed's soiled sheets in preparation for the next liaison. This would go on all afternoon. When she arrived back at her cramped apartment at the end of the day, Julio would silently watch as she kneeled in her maid's uniform before the crucifix that hung on the living room wall. Forgive me, Lord, she prayed. Forgive me for being a part of such wickedness. Please allow me to find an honorable way to make a living. And please watch over Julio and I.

Her prayers had been answered.

In the adjacent bedroom, she heard her son stirring.

Time to get up, she told herself as she swung her chubby legs to the floor. My boy has a big day ahead of him. He's going to need a good breakfast.

END.

Michael G. Vail

Earlier in my life my profession was that of a writer and editor. For the last 34 years, I have managed facility planning and construction programs at some of California's largest school districts.

Made in the USA
Las Vegas, NV
24 February 2021

18519949R00121